ALL IN A DAY'S WORK

Longarm couldn't believe it when the shooter, having emptied his six-gun, yanked a second pistol out of his waistband.

"Damn you!" Longarm bellowed. "I'm a United States marshal! Drop that gun!"

Now the maniac finally heard Longarm. He twisted around in his saddle and spurred his horse forward in a desperate attempt to run Longarm down and then make his escape. Longarm's hand flashed to his six-gun and brought it up taking a steady aim. "Stop or I'll shoot!"

But the horseman had no intention of stopping. So Longarm winged the horseman and then pistol-whipped him as his horse galloped past.

The wounded rider flipped over backward . . .

TABOR EVANS

LONGARM

AND THE
REBEL EXECUTIONER

J

JOVE BOOKS, NEW YORK

LONGARM AND THE REBEL EXECUTIONER

A Jove Book / published by arrangement with
the author

PRINTING HISTORY
Jove edition / November 1997

The Putnam Berkley World Wide Web site address is
http://www.berkley.com

ISBN: 0-515-12178-9

A JOVE BOOK®
Jove Books are published by The Berkley Publishing Group,
a member of Penguin Putnam Inc.,
200 Madison Avenue, New York, New York 10016.
JOVE and the "J" design are trademarks
belonging to Jove Publications, Inc.

PRINTED IN THE UNITED STATES OF AMERICA

10 9 8 7 6 5 4 3 2 1

LONGARM

AND THE
REBEL EXECUTIONER

Chapter 1

U.S. Deputy Marshal Custis Long was on his way to his office, located in the Federal Building, when he saw a small and ugly little dog jump out of the arms of a pretty young woman and dash into busy Colfax Avenue. The dog was some kind of a terrier, the yipping, aggressive kind that was a nuisance rather than an actual physical threat. Teeth bared, it had apparently taken an extreme dislike to a pinto ridden by a large, disreputable-looking man wearing a rumpled brown suit and a soiled derby hat.

"Get out of here!" the man yelled when his horse began to become fractious as the terrier nipped at its heels. "Get that goddamn mutt out of the street before I shoot it!"

The young woman cried out in alarm and ran headlong into the street after her dog. She was almost run over by a carriage that was traveling way too fast. In fact, the rear wheel of the carriage sideswiped the young lady and knocked her down hard. Longarm began to sprint across the street, hoping to grab the woman before she was either trampled or run over and crushed to death.

Everything was in chaos. The pedestrians on both sides of the street who had seen the woman were shouting, the damned terrier was barking like crazy, and the horseman was reaching for his side arm. Longarm's full concentration was on the fallen woman, who was obviously dazed and in great peril. A huge freight wagon barely missed the prostrate woman, and Longarm just managed to drag her out of the path of its iron-rimmed rear wheels. Scooping the lady up in his arms, he darted through the congested traffic and made his way to the sidewalk. The woman's temple was bruised and already starting to swell, but even so, she was very pretty, with dark brown hair and a heart-shaped face. Longarm judged her to be about twenty-five. From her dress, he supposed she was fairly well-to-do.

"Miss, are you all right?"

"What?" she asked in a daze.

"I said, are you all right?"

Her eyes fluttered open and she seemed to have some trouble focusing for several seconds. Then, her gloved hand flew to her face and she cried, "Prince!"

"Who?"

"Prince!"

The woman struggled to come to her feet, but she was still too dizzy to stand and collapsed back into the deputy's arms. "Don't let that man kill Prince!" she cried.

Longarm had never been much of a dog lover, especially when it came to the small, nasty-natured kind, but it was very obvious that this young lady held the dog in high regard. So he glanced up at one of the gawking spectators and said, "Watch her for a moment while I go rescue Prince."

But just as Longarm was turning to go after the stupid dog, he heard gunshots. Three of the them, to be exact. He looked up to see that the rider had opened fire on Prince right in the middle of that busy street.

"You gawddamn fool!" Longarm shouted. "Are you out of your mind?"

But the man was insane with anger, and kept firing at Prince out of sheer cussedness. The terrier was mortally wounded, but the horseman kept shooting. One of his slugs ricocheted off the cobblestones and struck a sorrel mare. The poor pain-maddened animal took off galloping down the street with its rider shouting, "Whoa! Whoa!"

Longarm couldn't believe his eyes when the shooter, after emptying his six-gun, yanked a second pistol out of his waistband and continued firing into the dead terrier's riddled body.

"Damn you!" Longarm bellowed. "I'm a United States marshal! Drop that gun! You are under arrest!"

Now the maniac finally heard Longarm. He twisted around in his saddle and spurred his horse forward in a desperate attempt to run Longarm down and then make his escape. Longarm's hand flashed to his six-gun and he brought it up taking a steady aim. "Stop or I'll shoot!"

But the horseman had no intention of stopping. Longarm supposed he could have shot the pinto and ended the affair without the loss of human life, but he didn't. Any man who would gun down a harmless dog and recklessly put human life in danger deserved to have a taste of his own medicine. And so, without even seeming to take aim, Longarm winged the horseman and then pistol-whipped him as his horse galloped past.

The wounded rider flipped over backward and his horse raced away, stirrups flapping. Longarm went over to the still and bloodied figure, then knelt at his side. The rider smelled like a distillery and when Longarm pulled open his coat, he saw that the fall had smashed a pint of whiskey, which was now mixing with blood from his bullet wound. The neck of the broken whiskey bottle was imbedded in his chest, and the rider was gasping for each and every breath.

"I'm Dr. Orvis Adams," a man of about fifty said. "Can I be of service?"

"I don't think so, but you can try to save him."

"He's bleeding like a stuck pig!"

"Yeah," Longarm agreed. "I'll stuff a handkerchief in the bullet hole. Meantime, why don't you go see if you can help the lady?"

"I've already examined her and she is going to be just fine."

"Then see if you can save Prince."

"Who?"

"Her dog!"

"The dog is dead. It's *this* patient that needs my immediate attention."

The doctor used his thumb to lift one of the man's eyelids, and then announced, "In addition to his obvious wounds, he's suffered a grievous head injury."

"You would be too if you got pistol-whipped."

"Marshal, we need to get him to my medical office right now!"

Longarm stood up. "One thing, Doc. If he lives, you make sure that *I* know about it because he'll be arrested for disturbing the peace and endangering life and property."

4

The doctor was seedy-looking, and it was clear that he hadn't bathed in quite a while. Longarm would have bet anything he wasn't even a real doctor, but simply a barber or tooth-yanker who was far more interested in a fat fee than in practicing good medicine.

"Marshal, how dare you think about arresting this man given his critical condition!"

"If he lives, he's going to spend at least two months in jail," Longarm said, ignoring the outburst.

"Marshal, I *resent* your calloused attitude toward this poor man's life!"

"Listen, Doc," Longarm growled, "because of this 'poor' man, as you call him, a little dog was riddled with bullets right here in the street and a foolish but otherwise innocent woman was almost killed. On top of that, this bastard wanted to run *me* down with his horse.

"And if all that wasn't enough, this jackass shot a saddle horse which ran off with its rider! So don't give me that crap about this 'poor' man!"

"Marshal, who is your superior? I intend to lodge a protest and make sure that you are severely reprimanded for your irresponsible attitude and behavior."

Longarm started to tell the doctor to go ahead and do whatever he wanted, but suddenly, the unconscious man began to quiver and emit a death rattle.

"Marshal, this man is dying!" the doctor declared.

"He just did," Longarm announced as the body went limp. "And to my way of thinking, instead of trying to figure out how to hang my ass, you should have been taking care of him. Maybe I'll lodge a protest against *you* to the medical society. That is, if you even belong to one."

Fear and apprehension quickly replaced indignation on the doctor's unshaven face.

"Well, Marshal," the man stammered, "perhaps we *both* might have handled this tragedy in a more professional manner. I'll . . . I'll send for an undertaker."

"Let's make sure that the State of Colorado doesn't get hooked for the funeral expenses, Doc."

Longarm quickly rifled through the dead man's pockets, but he found no cash or identification. Only the two six-guns and a cheap pocket watch.

"I'll take these," Longarm decided, "as well as his horse and saddle, which will be sold to cover his funeral expenses. If there's anything left, it will be given to the deceased's next of kin . . . if they come forward."

"Marshal, what about restitution for my medical services?"

"Doc, you didn't do a damned thing! The dog is dead, the woman is just bruised, and you let this bastard croak without lifting a finger except for the one you pointed at me. Go get an undertaker and quit while you're still ahead."

The doctor made a huffing sound to convey his displeasure, and then he hurried away. Longarm was now positive that the man had been a charlatan.

"Someone go find me an undertaker," he shouted at the gawking crowd. "Tell him I'll leave this fella on the corner of Cherokee."

Longarm grabbed the dead man's wrists and dragged his body over to the gutter by the corner. He found a newspaper and laid it across his face, then got the street cleared and the downtown traffic moving again. By that time some Denver policemen had arrived, and Longarm quickly filled them in on what had happened. Someone had already carried the little dog off the street.

It was now almost four o'clock in the afternoon, and Longarm knew he was going to catch hell from Billy for being late. That being the case, he decided to check on the young woman one last time.

She was almost fully recovered, but obviously very distraught over losing her dog. "Prince was such a wonderful little friend," she sniffled. "He would have given his *life* to protect me!"

"Yeah, but this afternoon, Prince almost *cost* you your life, Miss. . . ."

"Lucy Martin." She used a lace handkerchief to wipe the tears from her pretty brown eyes. "I shouldn't have brought Prince downtown today. He was in such a terrible mood. It's really all my fault."

"How do you figure?" Longarm asked. "I saw Prince jump out of your arms and dash into the street to attack that pinto. Why'd he take such a big dislike to that particular animal?"

"He's never been very friendly toward horses, and he has always hated pintos and paints."

"Why?"

"I imagine he was either kicked . . . or perhaps bitten by a pinto when he was a puppy. What other reason could there be?"

"None that I can think of," Longarm said, helping Lucy to her feet. "Well, Miss Martin, if you're all right, then I guess that I will be getting along now."

She swooned and leaned against his chest for support. Longarm didn't mind. The woman was lovely and smelled like roses. "I . . . I don't suppose you would help me get Prince home where I could bury him properly?"

"Do you live very far from here?" he asked. "I'm already late for a meeting."

"Only two blocks south."

"All right," he agreed. "Let me find something to

7

wrap the little fella's carcass in so that I don't ruin my clothes.''

"Thank you!''

Longarm went over to the dead man and removed his suit coat. It was blood-soaked on the inside. He wrapped little Prince's torn body in the coat and escorted Lucy a few blocks to her house.

"You must have married a very successful attorney or someone like that,'' Longarm said, admiring the stately two-story Victorian mansion.

"Oh, my father bought it for me a few years ago,'' Lucy explained. "He had intended to leave New York City and live here with me, but he had a heart attack and died on the train while crossing Nebraska.''

Longarm laid Prince on the stairs and shielded Lucy with his body from the sight of her dog. "So where is your mother?''

"She ran off with my father's young Greek valet and caught a boat headed for the Mediterranean. I learned later that it and everyone aboard were lost in a storm,'' Lucy explained, looking for all the world as though she was going to burst into tears again. "So now I live here with Mrs. Harney, my friend as well as maid and cook. She's fussy, but forgiving of everything I do. I love her very much.''

"Then you at least have someone.''

"Everyone needs *someone,* Marshal. Prince was my constant companion. He never expected much. I found him abandoned in the alley when he was just a puppy, and he repaid me with years of loyalty and love.''

"I'm genuinely sorry he's gone.''

Lucy expelled a ragged breath. "I have known great sadness in my life. Losing Prince is just the latest cruel misfortune. I am beginning to wonder if my entire life isn't cursed.''

"I very much doubt that," Longarm said, mounting the wide veranda and then escorting Lucy to the front door. "At least you have no complaints in respect to material comforts."

"Surely you know that they are meaningless without love and affection." She took his hands in her own and gazed deeply into his eyes. "Marshal, you are very, very brave and handsome."

Longarm could feel his cheeks warm, and decided it was time to say good-bye. "Miss Martin, I'd better go now."

"Please call me Lucy. After all, I owe you my life."

"I was just doing my job."

"I should *never* have allowed Prince to go shopping with me today. But he had chewed up his leash and I was going to the saddle shop to buy him a new one."

"I really need to go now," Longarm repeated.

"Please come in and keep me company for a short while. I'm very upset and I desperately need your quiet strength and presence."

Longarm had never been able to refuse a lady, especially one as pretty as Miss Lucy Martin. So he removed his hat and followed her inside and down a marble-floored hallway lined with oil paintings.

"My," he said, "this is *quite* the place."

"I suppose," Lucy said with an indifferent shrug. "But without Prince, I. . . ."

Lucy couldn't finish. Longarm saw fresh tears, and it was then he realized that even he felt damned bad about Prince. Sure, the dog had been worthless, and was directly responsible for all the harm that had been done, but it hadn't deserved to be riddled with bullets.

Longarm had owned plenty of dogs in his childhood, and he recalled one about the size and temperament of Prince who had been sleeping under his father's buckboard wagon when it started off down the road. The memory of that devastating boyhood loss still caused him a sharp stab of pain.

"I'm sure that you can find another nice little dog to replace Prince," he said, trying to console the grieving woman. "There's lots of them just runnin' wild and hungry in the streets of Denver. I could probably even scare up a pup for you."

"Marshal, let's not stand on formalities. What is your first name?"

"Custis."

"That fits you so well."

"It's just a name."

"Oh, but names are very important. For example, I could never think of you as a Charles or . . . heaven forbid, a Mortimer. And I have often thought that there are far too many Williams and Johns. Wouldn't you agree?"

"I never gave it much thought."

"Well, you should! I can spot a William, John, or Edward every time."

Longarm was trying desperately to think of an intelligent response when an older woman wearing an apron appeared. When she saw Lucy's red and puffy eyes, she exclaimed, "Miss Martin, are you all right?"

"We've had a tragedy, Miss Harney. Prince is dead."

"No!"

"I'm afraid so. And *I'd* be dead too if it wasn't for this wonderful United States marshal who saved my life and . . . and killed the lunatic that shot Prince!"

Mrs. Harney's lower lip trembled. "Is our dear little friend really gone?"

"I'm afraid so," Longarm said. "The little fella took such a dislike to a horse that he dashed into the street. The animal's crazy rider shot him plumb to pieces."

A sob escaped Mrs. Harney, but she managed to say, "You both could probably use a couple of strong drinks. I'll bring them to you in the parlor."

Longarm started to explain that he had a meeting with Billy Vail, but then he decided to hell with the meeting. It was already quitting time, and Longarm doubted that he could even get back to the Federal Building before it emptied. So he guided Lucy into the parlor, which boasted an impressive library and a big bearskin rug on the floor as well as several trophy-sized deer, bighorn sheep, and elk heads mounted on the walls.

Mrs. Harney returned with a bottle of very expensive brandy and two crystal glasses, which she filled to the brim. "I'll be taking a few nips in the kitchen, Miss Martin, while I prepare dinner. Will the marshal be staying?"

"Of course," Lucy said. "He saved my life. Do you think I could let him go without such a small repayment?"

"You don't owe me a thing," Longarm said, meaning it. "I'll just have a shot or two of that brandy and then be on my way."

"Absolutely not," Lucy insisted. "Unless. . . ."

"Unless what?"

"Unless you have a wife who will be expecting you?"

"I'm not married. My work is long on travel and usually dangerous. That's why I never think of marriage. It wouldn't be fair to a lady."

"How . . . how *very* thoughtful of you, Custis. You're not only brave, but thoughtful and kind."

11

Longarm wasn't accustomed to receiving such genuine compliments, especially from a lady like Lucy. "Here, Lucy," he said, taking the decanter of brandy and the crystal snifters. "Let me pour."

"To the top, Custis. I *really* need a strong drink."

"Me too."

They forgot about dinner, and began to talk about more pleasant things. It turned out that Lucy had inherited quite a lot of money, but it was kept in a trust back in Boston and she received a generous check each and every month.

"I do what little I can for the local charities," Lucy modestly explained. "And I spend a lot of time doing volunteer work because it helps to pass the time."

"Do you mind if I ask why you aren't married?"

"I was, once," Lucy said. "Victor was extremely charming and very handsome, but he was deceitful and such a beast! It soon became clear to me that Victor was after my money."

"That's a shame."

"Yes, but it wasn't long before I got rid of him."

"How?"

Lucy's eyes turned hard and bright as they peered over the top of her brandy snifter and she said, "Since you're a *law* officer, I'd rather not discuss Victor's sudden and extremely violent ending. All right?"

"Why, sure," he stammered. "I was just making conversation."

"Well," Lucy said, an edge creeping into her voice, "it's a very sore subject. I can say with certainty that the philandering brute will never again deceive a trusting young woman and attempt to steal her rightful inheritance."

Longarm couldn't help but wonder about Victor. "Has he been gone long?"

"Not nearly long enough."

"Dinner is ready!" Mrs. Harney announced.

The meal was splendid: asparagus, roast veal, and an excellent red wine, followed by apple pie for dessert. Afterward, they adjourned to the parlor, where Mrs. Harney brought them a second bottle of brandy even better than the first.

Longarm was really enjoying Lucy's company. She seemed to have completely recovered from losing Prince, and was now smiling and laughing. Maybe he was a little bit vain, but Longarm liked to think that he'd helped Lucy get her through this tragedy and back in high spirits.

"Good night," Mrs. Harney said, discreetly closing the door so that they could be alone.

"Custis, there's wood in that box and it would be very nice and cozy to have a fire," Lucy suggested, laying her hand on his thigh.

All the food, wine, and brandy, as well as the nearness of Lucy, was already making Longarm perspire. "But Lucy, it's warm in here."

"I know, but I just *love* a fire, a handsome man, and this imported Italian brandy. Would you mind catering to my wishes just this one evening?"

"No," Longarm said, jumping to his feet and grabbing wood from the firebox. It didn't take him any time at all to get the fire started.

"You do that very well," Lucy said, her voice the tiniest bit slurred. "I bet you do *everything* well."

Longarm was down on the floor fanning the fire when he felt Lucy's hand slip around his chest and slide between the buttons of his shirt.

"What. . . ."

"No one has ever risked his own life to save mine," Lucy breathed as her lips brushed the back of his neck. "Custis, I want to do something very, very *special* to repay you."

"Here?"

"Why not?"

Longarm couldn't think of a single damned reason. "Well, Lucy, it's just that you sort of surprised me and . . ."

Lucy didn't give him time to finish. With far more strength than Longarm would have imagined, she pushed him over and attacked him as if she were a starving animal.

"Custis," she panted as she unbuttoned his shirt and began to kiss his chest and lightly pinch his nipples, "I believe that making love is the best medicine for dealing with sorrow, don't you?"

"It sure can't hurt!"

Lucy undressed them both far quicker than any lady Longarm had ever known. She took his manhood and rolled it back and forth between her soft, silky palms until it stood at attention. With a sigh of pleasure, Lucy impaled herself upon him. Sighing deeply, she began to move up and down in a way that Longarm knew would soon drive him wild.

Longarm studied her with half-closed eyes. Lucy was an enigma. A lady in public, but secretly, a wildcat. Her breasts were large and firm and her lovemaking was exceptional. Longarm could not help but wonder how Lucy had ever learned how to make love so well. Then he remembered Victor. Lucy had admitted that her former husband was a notorious philanderer, and Longarm supposed that he had taught his young wife all the ways that a man and a woman could make exciting and passionate love.

"Do you like this?" she whispered, smiling in firelight which turned her body the color of liquid gold.

"I like this," he told her with a big smile.

Lucy purred like a big, contented cat as her bottom moved up and down harder and quicker, until Longarm reached up and grabbed her hips, then rolled her over on the bearskin rug.

Her fingernails raked his buttocks and he grimaced. "Take it easy!"

Longarm was shocked and surprised at her wanton behavior, but he sure wasn't complaining as the woman threw back her head and growled like a wildcat. Bathed by firelight, her breasts were beaded with golden globules of perspiration. The breasts were big and firm, and Longarm had a taste of them, causing Lucy to purr with pleasure.

"Honey, I want it *hard*!"

Longarm was more than willing to oblige. The bearskin rug was deep and it felt just dandy. He crushed Lucy's lips and sucked on her breasts while their bodies surged in and out like two great tides. Soon, Longarm's lips were drawn back and he was growling as his big rod plunged very deep in Lucy's wet womanhood a moment before he stiffened and began spewing his hot seed.

Chapter 2

When Longarm finally stumbled into Marshal Billy Vail's office the next morning, his boss shouted, "Jeezus, Custis, you look like you been run down and whipped! Where in the hell have you been?"

"I'm sorry about missing our meeting yesterday afternoon," Longarm answered, collapsing in a chair across the desk from Billy. "I almost made it here, but then there was some trouble out in the street."

"Yeah, I heard that you had no choice but to shoot some crazy bastard."

"And pistol-whip him," Longarm admitted. "He was shooting the street up and it's damn fortunate that a bunch of innocent people weren't killed."

"There were a lot of witnesses, so you've got nothing to worry about. What happened to the lady that was knocked down by the wagon?"

"Well," Longarm said, knuckling his bloodshot eyes, "that was sort of the reason I wasn't quite able to get back here to the office before closing time."

"Was she hurt?"

"Oh, yeah!"

Billy waited, and when Longarm didn't offer to tell him any more, he said, "And I suppose you, being the charming Southern gentleman that you are, had to escort her to a doctor."

"The man I shot killed her little dog, Billy. It was a real mess and she was very upset."

"I see."

Billy drummed his desk top with his stubby fingertips. In contrast to Longarm, who stood well over six feet tall and was in his physical prime, Billy Vail was short and almost dumpy. But Longarm knew that Billy had once been an excellent deputy marshal, and was still far tougher and quicker than he appeared. Billy was smart and resourceful and he understood the criminal mind, which made him an exceptional lawman. A little older and softer now, Billy had demonstrated his mettle dozens of times, and could do so again if he ever decided to take a pay cut and stop riding a plush office chair.

"Longarm, are you just going to come right out with it and admit that you *didn't* take her to the doctor, but took her to bed instead?"

"I'm not going to admit anything of the kind," Longarm said. "A gentleman never talks of such things."

A thin smile lifted the corners of Billy's mouth. "Oh, you don't have to tell me. I can see it in your sleep-starved, watery eyes. You took the poor girl home and that's where you stayed last night."

"You're just guessing, Billy."

"I sent someone over to your place and you never showed," Billy said. "And I also know that you weren't back this morning when I walked past your place to work."

"What were we supposed to have a meeting about?" Longarm asked, wanting to change the subject.

"You should settle down with a good woman and get married," Billy advised.

"Oh, yeah? If I were foolish enough to do that, which I'm not, I'd sink to politicking for *your* desk job, which I'd hate but feel bound to ask for because I'd have a carping wife threatening to leave me if I didn't stick around Denver more."

"You're right." Billy leaned back in his chair and laced his fingers behind his head. "A promotion is a real trap. Most of the fun and the interesting jobs take place out in the field. I make better money than I ever expected, and get to take it home to my wife, but *you* get to ride off into the sunset on one hair-raising adventure after another."

"You had your time," Longarm said, starting to feel better. "No one forced you into a desk job with a nice office and bigger paycheck."

"No one except my family responsibilities," Billy said. "Oh, well, everything in life has a price. Nothing is free, and even our *rewards* always have a price. Sometimes we don't see it until it's too late, but it's there."

"What is it that you want, Billy? Why the deep philosophical questions? Is something eating at you?"

Billy's genial smile evaporated. "Actually, there is something that has been eating at me like a cancer. It's something that I first thought was just a series of coincidences, then later began to view with growing alarm. And now . . . now I'm convinced I'm on to something that is really quite chilling."

Longarm raised his eyebrows. "Oh? Come on, Billy!

You know me well enough to understand that you don't have to build up a case. If you need a job done, I'll go. Now, there are places I'd rather *not* go, but I'll go. What is it this time?''

Billy reached into his desk and retrieved a thick brown manila folder. Setting it carefully on his desk, he opened it to show Longarm that it was filled with newspaper clippings. Some of them were beginning to turn yellow, so Longarm figured Billy had been amassing this file for quite a while.

"What have we got?" Longarm asked, reaching into his pocket and pulling out a cheap cheroot, which he stuffed into his mouth without bothering to light it.

"Take this file straight to your desk and study it for an hour or two," Billy ordered. "I want you to read every article and then explain to me how you think they are connected."

Longarm turned the file around and began thumbing through the newspaper articles, glancing at their headlines. Every single one was about someone's untimely death or fatal accident. In less than a minute, Longarm had seen enough to understand that these tragic and unusual deaths had all taken place in Arizona, California, and Nevada.

"Billy, why are you collecting obituaries?"

"I collect clues, and that's how I reach sound conclusions. But before I tell you what those articles indicate to me, I want you to reach your *own* conclusions. If yours and mine are the same, I'm putting you on a westbound train."

"In case you have forgotten," Longarm drawled, "the West is a very big piece of real estate. Are you thinking of sending me to any *specific* part of it, or am

I just supposed to jump off when my train ticket runs out?''

''Don't try and be funny, Custis, because you are not and you never will be. Just take the damned file and read it.''

''Reading obituaries is not my idea of fun.''

Billy wasn't listening. ''We'll meet at noon and go to lunch somewhere quiet where we can talk without being overheard.''

''You're actually going to buy?'' Longarm asked.

''I didn't say that.''

''Then let's meet right here and skip lunch.''

''All right,'' Billy said, ''I'll buy. Be here at noon. Don't go outside the office. Is that understood?''

''Sure, but I could use a few more cigars and. . . .''

''No,'' Billy said. ''You can get them at noon. Read the damned file and tell me what you think . . . if you have anything left to think with after last night.''

Longarm yawned. ''I *could* use a pot of coffee. Is Alice still making it for us?''

''Not for you,'' Billy said. ''Not since you screwed her that evening on your desk and she couldn't bend over for three weeks because she wrenched her back.''

''I feel real bad about that,'' Longarm admitted. ''But Alice was in kind of a hurry and. . . .''

''Spare me the details! Now, get out of here and I'll make the damned coffee myself and bring it by for you.''

''Really!'' Longarm came to his feet grinning. ''Why, Billy, this case must be pretty damned bad if you're willing to make *my* coffee.''

''Git!''

Longarm started for the door, and was passing out into the main office when Billy called out, ''Longarm just

21

answer me one question. Did you bury her dog, or just bury your wick?''

''Shut up,'' Longarm snapped as he headed for his desk hoping that Billy really knew how to make decent coffee.

He had the file open and was starting to read the first newspaper article even before he sank into his beat-up old office chair. Longarm's desk was the worst in the building. One of its legs was busted, and he'd had to support it with some books. The desk was scarred, and so old that no one could even remember where it came from. Probably from a Washington, D.C., government surplus sale.

The first obituary reported the strange demise of Colonel Michael Lowe, a highly decorated Union officer who, on August 29 and 30, 1862, had kept his company of Union soldiers from retreating at the Second Battle of Bull Run and had inflicted heavy casualties on the Confederate troops before falling back with the rest of General Pope's forces.

After the war, Colonel Lowe had gone west and bought himself a cattle ranch just outside of Prescott, Arizona. Hard working, industrious, and intelligent, he'd built a small ranch into a cattle empire, and had announced his intention to run for the Territorial Legislature when his ranch house had burned down, killing not only himself but his wife and three children. The cause of the fire was unknown, and it remained a mystery why at least some of the family hadn't been able to escape since some of their bedrooms were situated on the first floor. Some of Lowe's cowboys had said that the house had just ''seemed to explode'' like a bomb.

''Humm,'' Longarm mused, skipping the last part of the obituary concerning the funeral details.

The second article was underlined where it read, "Captain Stanley Otterman was already a highly decorated Union officer in the battle of Antietam Creek on September 17 when General McClellan's army was able to stop the advance of General Robert E. Lee's invasion of the North." Captain Otterman had been so heroic that his troops had outfought the Confederate forces and Otterman himself had been awarded the Medal of Honor.

During the Battle of Fredricksburg, Virginia, eighteen-year-old corporal William Treadwell had also won the Medal of Honor by infiltrating the Confederate lines and gaining valuable military information on the attack plans of General Lee. While in Lee's camp, he had donned a Confederate uniform and killed five enemy sentries. Unfortunately, Treadwell had been observed trying to escape, and had been severely wounded before he could return to the Union lines. And even though the battle was a major victory for the Confederacy, Treadwell's superiors had recognized that it would have even been a greater disaster for the North if not for the young corporal's heroics. For this act of extreme bravery, Treadwell had been given the rank of captain, and had then gone on to distinguish himself in many battles.

Treadwell had also come west, and although he had not achieved either fame or fortune, he had written several books on his role in the Civil War and become quite a celebrity in Tucson, Arizona. Unfortunately, he and his family had all died of apparent food poisoning. They had been found slumped over their kitchen table with ghastly expressions on their faces.

Robert Shaw had distinguished himself as a Union artillery officer, serving at the Battle of Chancellorsville and then one month later at the Battle of Gettysburg, when his company had helped to repel the gallant but futile charge of Confederate General George Pickett's troops on July 3, 1863. Tragically, Shaw had been found hanging by a rope, an apparent suicide, in Reno, Nevada.

In Bodie, California, George Blair, another Union officer who had won the coveted Medal of Honor, had lost his own life and that of his wife and daughter when a wheel on their wagon had mysteriously detached while in motion. The wagon had flipped over and hadn't been discovered for nearly a week. By then, the bodies of the three were badly decomposed, but an undertaker had said that it looked like Mr. Blair had been strangled, with fingerlike imprint bruises still evident around his neck. In addition, the necks of his wife and daughter appeared to have been rope-burned.

Longarm was feeling very uneasy and depressed by noon, and was certainly in no mood for lunch. This was, he supposed, exactly why Billy had offered to take him. Even so, they went out to a cafe and found a private booth.

"I'll have a beer," Billy said, studying Longarm's grim expression. "What will you have, Custis?"

"Rye whiskey. Make it a double."

The waiter nodded and hurried off. It wasn't until their drinks were delivered and consumed and another round ordered that Billy said, "Well, I see that your reaction to those newspaper articles is every bit as somber as my own. What do you make of them?"

Longarm shrugged. "They were all either Union officers or enlisted men who became heroes during battle. They came from many different backgrounds, but they all met violent deaths in the West."

"Yes, and they were in good, I might even say vigorous, health. And what about the ones that either were or appeared to be strangled or hanged?"

"I don't know," Longarm admitted. "In every single article that I read, the deaths were unexplained and unnatural. Each man suffered a very, very violent ending, and the worst of it is that their families often suffered the same fate."

"Well, now, Longarm," Billy said, his face becoming almost animated because of his mounting excitement. "You've stated the obvious. The victims were all Civil War heroes for the North. What else?"

"They won their fame in battles that took place in the same general time and place. Also, quite a few of them won the Medal of Honor, the North's highest battlefield decoration."

"Exactly! *Now* are you beginning to see what I see?"

"No, and I think that you are really grabbing at straws, Billy."

"Am I? How many obituaries and articles did you read? How many victims?"

"Must have been more than twenty, I guess."

"And *all highly decorated Union soldiers*! Doesn't that strike you as just a little too coincidental?"

Longarm finished his second drink. Now he knew exactly what Billy wanted him to do. But dammit, where could he even start?

"All right," Longarm agreed, "it is highly unusual, but the West is a violent place."

"I'm not buying that and neither are you."

"Billy, these gents resettled all over the West! And I saw no connection between them after the war was over. They didn't know each other. They didn't keep in contact, and they didn't even seem to have the same friends."

"We don't know that for sure," Billy argued. "And

they didn't relocate *all* over the West. They all died in either California, Nevada, or Arizona.''

"That's a lot of country, Boss."

"Yes, but . . . well, maybe they had a Civil War reunion and that was how they were connected."

"Nope," Longarm said. "I don't think so."

"Why not?"

"Because some of them became rich and prominent while others never achieved much after the Civil War."

"I still believe they are all connected," Billy said, setting his jaw. "I believe it so strongly that I've brought it to the attention of my superiors."

"Why are *you* so caught up in this mystery?"

Billy looked away for a moment, and then he turned back to Longarm. "Custis, Robert Shaw was a distant cousin, and his sister Carole sent me these articles. According to her, someone is *executing* Union heroes. One by gawdamn one. She works for a newspaper and just happened to chance upon the connection. Not knowing who else to turn to, and getting no support or interest from the local authorities, she made up that file and sent it to me last week."

Longarm fired up his cheroot. "All right," he said, "let's agree that this does look highly suspicious and that there are far too many connections and similarities in these deaths to be accounted for by mere chance."

"Of course there are," Billy agreed.

"So what has this to do with our *federal* department?"

Billy didn't bat an eyelash when he drawled, "Absolutely nothing."

Longarm almost dropped his cigar. "Then . . . then what business or authority have I to investigate?"

Billy leaned forward, though for what reason Longarm could not imagine. The cafe was a noisy, boisterous place, and Billy would have had to have shouted to be overheard. "Custis, I took this matter to the bureau chief and he passed it on to the President, who wants us to investigate."

"The President of these United States?"

"That's right," Billy said. "These unfortunate dead men were *all* highly decorated Union soldiers and the President thinks that the least we can do—if there is *any* possibility of a murderer at work here—is to investigate and to *eliminate* the guilty party or parties."

"You mean *kill* them?"

"That's right. To arrest and bring such a monster or monsters to trial would incite passions and divisions best left sleeping."

"They're not sleeping, Billy. I have been to Dixie since the war, and the passions and hatreds run as deep as ever."

"I know," Billy said. "So try to imagine what would happen in the South if a killer of Union war heroes was arrested and brought to trail."

"It would open old wounds."

"You bet it would, Custis! Because we're talking about some crazy bastard who has a personal vendetta and is systematically wiping out Union Medal of Honor recipients and their *innocent families*! Why, the war between the North and the South would start up all over again!"

"Oh, come on, Billy."

"All right, maybe I am exaggerating. But you know it would result in a flare-up of old animosities. The battle lines would be drawn once more, Northerner against Southerner. Initially, I expect, there'd be just skirmishes here and there, but maybe those isolated skirmishes

27

would trigger more widespread violence, and pretty soon *lots and lots* of good people would be dying.''

Billy leaned back in his seat. ''Custis, the President can't afford to take that chance. This country is just starting to heal, and if the national press got a hold of this story, they'd fan the flames and I'm telling you that there would be murder and mayhem.''

''Okay,'' Longarm said quietly. ''I believe you. You've never lied to me before and. . . .''

''And I never will,'' Billy promised. ''My bureau chief asked me to recommend the best man for the job, and I didn't have to give the matter any thought to come up with your name.''

''I ought to be flattered instead of feeling like I've somehow been suckered.''

''You *have* been flattered, Custis. There *is* a crazed and deadly man or group of assassins out there someplace in California or Arizona or Nevada. Maybe in all three. I don't know how in the world you or anyone else could track them down, but if anyone can, it's you.''

''Don't patronize me, boss. This is going to be a damn near impossible job. We don't even know where to start looking for this fanatic . . . or bunch of fanatics.''

''That's right, but will you do it?''

''Did you already give my name to the President?''

''No. I wanted to talk to you first. He was expecting to hear from me yesterday, and I would have sent a message last night if you hadn't got involved with that dog woman.''

''She's not a 'dog woman,' dammit!''

''I don't care what she is,'' Billy said. ''Do I have your permission to offer the President of the United States *your* name?''

''Buy me one more whiskey and you can even give

him my pocket watch as well," Longarm said cryptically.

"Don't be insulting to the President."

"All right," Longarm said. "I'll take the case. When do you want me to leave?"

"How about on the first train west? It departs at five o'clock tomorrow afternoon." Billy reached into his inside coat pocket. "Here's your ticket."

"Where does it take me to?"

"Wherever you want to go," Billy said. "It's an open ticket for any railroad in the country, and as you can see, it's signed by the President. Show it to the conductor and he'll give you a first-class compartment. All your meals will be paid. This afternoon I'll have your expense money."

"How much?"

"A thousand dollars. I also have a letter from the President authorizing you unlimited funds at any federally chartered bank to be drawn on the United States Government up to five thousand additional dollars."

Longarm emitted a low whistle of surprise. "My gawd, Billy! I can't believe what I'm hearing."

"You're to remain in the field until you catch and kill this Rebel executioner."

"You're pretty sure he's a Reb?"

"Of course. Aren't you?"

"Yeah," Longarm said. "Who else?"

Billy ordered them a big lunch then, and explained by saying, "Custis, you look terrible. You're too thin and you've been drinking and screwing too many women instead of getting healthful sleep."

"No," Longarm countered, "I've been *working* too hard. I haven't had a vacation in. . . ."

"Solve this case for our department and the President

and I promise you a month . . . no, three months off at full pay.''

"Seriously?"

"You've got my word on it. And I'll tell you something else. If you handle this the way only you can, you'll be offered a huge promotion. Why, you might even become *my* direct superior.''

"I couldn't do that any more than I'd want to take your desk job. But Billy, I do have a question and I expect a straight answer.''

"Ask.''

"Why didn't *you* request this case for yourself?''

Billy studied his hands, and it was quite a long while before he said, ''Because, the truth of it is that I don't think I'm equal to the assignment.''

"Aw, come on!''

"I'm serious! I've read those obituaries and articles dozens of times, and whoever is doing this has got to be a stone-hearted killer without a shred of a conscience. He or they would have to be extremely ruthless and cunning and absolutely brutal. You can tell that because of the families they've also murdered!''

"Yeah.''

"Get them!'' Billy swore with passion. "Find him or them and *kill* them just as you would a scorpion or a viper! Kill them before they kill any more women, children, and war heroes.''

"I'll do my level best, but I don't even know where the trail should begin.''

"Start by calling on my cousin. Talk to Carole. She may have found more victims, and if some are recently murdered, you'll have a warm trail.''

"That makes sense."

"If it does," Billy said biting into a beef and cheese sandwich on sourdough bread which had just been delivered, "it's the *only* thing that does."

Chapter 3

Longarm had some mixed emotions as he left his office late that afternoon with one thousand dollars of government expense money, a train ticket that would take him anywhere he wanted to go in the United States of America, and the President's written authority to do whatever was necessary in order to eliminate what they were now all calling the Rebel Executioner.

On the one hand, he was extremely proud that his name had been chosen above all others for this important mission, but on the other hand, he had never imagined he would be sent out to assassinate an assassin. What he had been asked to do was to step outside the law and take the law into his own hands. Sure, the stakes were extremely high, and the end would probably justify the means, but killing without the benefit of a trial by judge or jury was murder.

So as Longarm packed his few belongings that night, and prepared to take the next day's train west to Reno, where he would meet Miss Carole Shaw, assistant editor for some Nevada newspaper, he was troubled. After all, what was he supposed to do when he found the Rebel Executioner? Just gun him down without warning? Ambush him like a coward or a cold-blooded killer?

Longarm had killed a lot of men, but never without cause, and often simply to save his own life. This, however, was very different. On the other hand, to warn this monster would be to risk his own life and the lives of who knows how many other Union Army heroes . . . and their families. Longarm didn't think he had the right to risk any more women and children, especially when he reread some of the shocking accounts of supposed "accidents" in which even small children were brutally killed.

Longarm went to bed alone and very early that night, but he lay awake until way past midnight thinking about how he might best accomplish this exceedingly difficult but also vital mission. Where would he start to look? The last obituary in the file sent by Carole Shaw was nearly four months old. But perhaps Miss Shaw had new incidents that would fit in with this killer's demented string of assassinations. Longarm hoped, yet dreaded, that this would be the case. It would mean that he would have a much fresher trail.

He awoke at seven o'clock the next morning feeling anything but rested. He made himself a pot of strong coffee, and then opened his front door to see if his morning paper had already been delivered. It hadn't, but Longarm didn't get upset over these things. He would have to leave a note telling the newspaper to stop delivery for an indefinite amount of time until he notified them of his return to Denver, which might be one hell of a long time.

Longarm shaved and bathed, then dressed, and was just about to go to the office when he heard a knock at his door. It would probably be Billy Vail wanting to discuss the case some more. Longarm had never seen his boss so obsessed with a case. Maybe, Longarm thought, Billy had even managed to talk his superiors into allowing him to also go west and help out on this one. Now, *that* would be very interesting.

"Coming, coming!" Longarm said, reaching for his six-gun more out of habit than a sense of danger. It was just that a lawman who had made as many enemies as he had could never let down his guard.

"Who is it?" Longarm asked as he paused inside his door.

"It's Lucy. Lucy Martin."

"Lucy?"

"Yes, open up, please! I feel ridiculous standing here talking to a door."

Longarm unbolted his lock and opened the door. Sure enough, Lucy was standing there as pretty as a sunrise, all smiles and smelling of roses.

"What are *you* doing here?"

Lucy swept inside. She looked over the room in a glance and then said, "How much do they pay you?"

"Not much."

"I can see that, Custis."

He was a little offended. "Well, I'm hardly ever in town anyway, so it doesn't matter."

"No," Lucy said, staring at a stack of dirty laundry piled on the hardwood floor, "I can see that."

"Did you come for a reason other than to tell me how badly I live?"

Lucy blushed and gave Longarm a hug. "I'm sorry,

but you were supposed to come back yesterday and see me. Custis, how could you forget?''

Longarm didn't remember any such promise. On the other hand, he'd had quite a bit of brandy and wine that night, and it was altogether possible that he'd promised to return to Lucy's mansion.

''I'm sorry,'' he said, ushering her inside. ''I've had my mind on other matters the past day and I'm. . . .''

Lucy's eyes fell on his half-packed suitcase and a carpetbag that he had recently bought for travel. ''Custis!'' she cried with alarm. ''Say you're not leaving me!''

''Not you,'' he said as she threw herself into his arms and squeezed his neck. ''I'm just leaving town for a while. I told you that I traveled quite a bit.''

''But . . . but you didn't say anything about having to leave so soon!''

''I didn't realize I would be,'' he replied, definitely feeling guilty because her eyes were misting with tears and he could tell that she was badly hurt and disappointed. ''Honestly, I just got this assignment, and it's so important that I have to leave on this afternoon's train.''

''Without even telling me!''

''I would have come by for a few minutes and told you,'' he said, doubting that this was true, but knowing he would have written or . . . or somehow gotten her word of his sudden departure, telling her he would see her again just as soon as he returned.

Lucy sniffled. ''You would have?''

''Sure!''

''What if I was out? I'm out a lot, Custis.''

''Then I'd have told Mrs. Harney.''

''Sometimes she goes with me.''

"Then I'd have written a *note* telling you the circumstances."

"Can't someone *else* do this job?" she asked imploringly. "You told me that you expected to be in Denver for at least a month because you'd been on assignment and traveling more than anyone else in your department."

"Well, that's true, but something really important has come up, Lucy. Something that can't be ignored."

"Murder?"

"We think so."

"Where?"

"I don't know."

Lucy stepped back and put her hands on her hips. "What do you mean, you don't know? How could you *not* know?"

"Lucy, it's a real complicated matter that might or might not involve murder. That's what I have to find out."

"Where are you going?"

"I'll be starting my investigation in Reno," he told her. "And after that, it's anyone's guess where I'll be headed."

"It sounds *really* exciting! I've always wanted to see Reno. I hear it's quite beautiful."

"At this time of year it's mostly just hot. You wouldn't like it right now."

"I'd like it *any* time of the year, as long as we were together."

"Absolutely not."

"Why not?"

"Because I'm going there on some very important business."

"I'll pay my own way and take care of myself. But

we could at least have fun riding out together and back on the train, couldn't we?''

Longarm could see where this was going, and the very last thing he wanted or needed was a lady friend tagging along as he untangled a brutal murderer's trail. "Lucy," he said, trying to be patient and kind, "it could be very dangerous."

"I'd love some danger in my life! I'm sick and tired of always living an easy, risk-free existence. And I even have a few acquaintances in Reno that I could visit. Oh, Custis, *please* let me come along with you!"

"Absolutely not."

Her eyes flashed with anger. "I don't see how you can stop me. I mean, this *is* a free country, is it not?"

"Yes, but . . ."

"I'm coming with you," she said, stomping her foot down hard on his floor. "And you really can't keep me from buying a ticket on this afternoon's train bound for Reno."

"I can't stop you," he agreed, feeling a rising anger and exasperation, "but I also can't encourage or even recommend that you come. Lucy, I'm going to try and track down a murderer. Maybe even more than one. I could be gone for months!"

"Then that is all the more reason why I should come along," she insisted. "I'm going to buy a ticket."

"You can't be ready to go by five o'clock! And even if you are, I'd ignore you all the way to Reno."

"Why?"

"I need to put all my attention on this case!"

"No," she countered, "you need to have someone to help you relax and to make sure that you eat well and get enough sleep."

38

"And *you're* going to come with me to help me get sleep? Lucy, don't be ridiculous!"

"All right," she said, "we'll just have to see how it goes. If I can't be a help and begin to have any idea at all that I'm a hindrance, I promise that I'll return to Denver on the first train."

"Lucy, please be reasonable! My job is very dangerous."

"If I don't go with you, I might never have a real adventure," she said, stomping her foot down hard again. "And besides, perhaps you'll even think of a way that I could be of service."

"Not a chance."

She opened her purse and dragged out a derringer. "I have never shot this, but I'm sure it's lethal."

Longarm took the gun from her hand. It wasn't even loaded, but it was a very fine two-shot .44-caliber with a real ivory handle and excellent workmanship.

"You don't have any bullets for it."

"Not with me, but I have some at home and I'll bring a fistful of them along."

Longarm knew that there was no point in further discussion. "Look," he said, "I have to do some errands and go by the office for a while. I was planning on stopping by to see you on my way to the train station early this afternoon."

"Don't bother," she said. "I'll just meet you at the station. If you like, we can stay with my old childhood friend. Her name is—"

"No," Longarm said. "I'll stay at the hotel down near the Truckee River where I always stay."

Lucy's eyes blinked rapidly, and he knew she was trying not to cry, especially when she said, "I don't know how we can make love two nights ago and then you can treat me this way, Custis.''

"I'm sorry, I really am. But I'm not going to let you get involved in this business. It's a particularly bad and difficult case.''

"And I'm a particularly stubborn woman," Lucy said as she whirled and headed for the door. "You just wait and see if the day doesn't come when you'll admit that you were wrong about not wanting me to come along. I may even just help *solve* your case and *catch* your crook.''

"He's not a crook. He's a cunning murderer who takes lives with no more thought than you would have of cutting flowers for a crystal vase. He's killed not only those he believes are his enemies, but also their entire *families*! By that I mean wives, sons, and daughters no matter how young or innocent.''

"You're not just saying all this to shock me, are you, Custis?''

"I only wish that I were.''

Lucy stopped by the door. "I fell in love with you, Custis. Or maybe I'm just in lust with you. Either way, I *have* to come along and see if there is something that I can do to help.''

"Dammit, the best help you could give me is to stay right here in Denver.''

"But who would protect me if someone almost runs me over in the street again, or tries to rob me or. . . .''

"Go home and stay home, Lucy.''

She whirled and left him, and Longarm felt like a rat because he could hear her sobbing as she rushed down the hallway. He closed his door, wondering if she would reconsider now that he had told her about the kind of man, or men, he was after.

"I sure hope so," he muttered as he went to finish his preparations for leaving.

An hour later, Longarm was back in Billy's office, sitting in the same chair and watching Billy pace nervously back and forth as he talked out his frustration. "I asked my superior if I could go with you on this one," he said. "My request was turned down."

"I'll be all right. Your place is here now, Billy."

"Doing what? Wearing out the carpet as I wonder how the hell you are getting along?"

"I'll send telegrams wherever and whenever I can," Longarm promised, knowing that he rarely would think to do so once he was immersed in the work.

"You'd *better*!" Billy vowed. "Because my boss will be asking about you on a daily basis, or at least an every-other-day basis, and I'd damn sure better have something to tell him."

"You won't," Longarm predicted. "You know this is going to take weeks, if not months, to figure out unless I get very, very lucky."

"Or my cousin Carole has something that can help you," Billy said, looking very upset. "Here, I've written a letter for you to give to her, and it's also got her address. I wouldn't recognize her if she walked through the door right now. It's been . . . oh, thirty years since we last saw each other, and we've only communicated at Christmas. Anyway, this letter is also sort of an introduction."

Longarm took the letter. "Thanks." He drew out his pocket watch and said, "Well, I guess I'll go to lunch."

"I'm buying again," Billy said, reaching for his hat. "Let's go."

"I don't know why you're buying when I'm carrying

41

all the government expense money. But if that's the way
you want it, then it's fine with me.''

''Hell, you're right. *You* buy the lunch.''

Longarm and Billy went to a good steak house and
had a fine meal. They didn't talk much. The talking time
was past, so they just enjoyed their sumptuous dinner in
relative silence. The entire affair would have been une-
ventful except for some loudmouthed sonofabitch at a
table not far away who was browbeating his wife for
just about everything imaginable.

They were an unlikely couple, both in their late twen-
ties. The husband was large and swarthy with wide shoulders and a foul mouth that rankled Longarm, while his
wife was, well, kind of plain, but pleasant enough on the
eye. She was small and proper-looking, and she was obviously in the habit of allowing herself to be bullied.

''Gawdammit, Clara, you just don't have any idea
how hard it is on me to keep paying all the bills on the
salary I'm earning! You got to start taking in some laundry or something!''

''But I'm already working all day and—''

''Shut up! You ain't making enough money. I make
damn near double what you're bringing in, and your
father hasn't done me any favors when he gave me the
job. I *hate* working for him!''

''John, please, if you'll only give Father a little more
time and just listen to what he has to say, you'd get
along so much better.''

''One of these days, I'm going to grab him by the
nape of his skinny neck, shove his face in the pickle
barrel, and hold it there till the sonofabitch is nearly
drowned.''

Clara covered her face with her napkin and burst into
tears. When John tried to tear the napkin from her hands,

Billy Vail jumped up, marched over, and clamped his chubby little fist on John's shoulder.

"I think you've made your point," Billy said in a voice as sharp as shattered glass. "Upsetting your wife isn't going to help matters."

John lunged to his feet, his face inflamed with anger. "Are you butting into *my* business, you fat little fart?"

"Damn right I am," Billy said.

Longarm started to come to his feet, but Billy waved him off, and so Longarm sat down again, eyes tight with anger.

John grinned and threw a punch at Billy, who ducked under it and slammed an uppercut to John's gut. Unfortunately, the bully was as hard as rawhide. He barely took a backward step, then grabbed Billy by the shirt-front and hurled him across the restaurant. Billy spilled over an empty table and came up fighting. He managed to land two solid punches, and one of them opened a nasty cut under the bully's right eye. But the man was just too big and strong, and he was a good twenty years Billy's junior. John hit Billy three times, and Longarm winced as his friend reeled backward and then dropped to the floor.

Clara was screaming for help and other diners were heading for the exits as Billy, his eyes glazed, struggled to his feet and tried to focus and attack.

"Boss, I'm sorry," Longarm said, coming out of his seat, "but sometimes a man has to ask for help."

"Help!" Billy croaked.

That was all the asking Longarm needed to hear. He wiped his lips with his napkin and stepped around his table to face the bully.

"You want some of the same that I gave to your fat fart friend, huh?"

43

"Yeah," Longarm said, balling his fists. "You've bullied your poor wife and whipped my friend, but I'm a lot closer to your size."

John tried to bury the toe of his boot in Longarm's groin. It was a good kick, plenty fast, but Longarm had seen that move too many times not to be prepared. Jumping back, he grabbed John's boot and heaved it straight up overhead, spilling the bully hard. Right then and there he could have ended the fight by kicking John in the balls, but instead, he just backed off and let the fool climb a bit unsteadily to his feet.

"You big sonofabitch, come on and fight!" John hissed, wading in with both fists.

Longarm blocked a swinging right and ducked an overhand left, then stepped in close and pounded his fists into John's gut. Longarm packed thunder in both fists, and now John's mouth flew open like a beached fish sucking poison air. Longarm could hear Clara wailing for them to stop fighting, but Billy was also yelling and he wanted Longarm to dismantle the foul-tempered sonofabitch.

With John's mouth hanging open, Longarm sledged a straight right cross that crashed into the big man's jaw and broke it with a sickening "pop." John howled and Longarm flattened his nose. He could have broken every bone in John's face, but instead, he supported the bully with his left hand, then began slapping John's bloody face until his eyes swelled shut and his lips were pink pulp.

"No more!" John babbled, covering his face and trying to support his broken jaw. "Please, no more!"

Longarm stopped inflicting his terrible punishment. "What's your full name!"

John tried to tell him, but couldn't.

44

"His name is John Truitt and he's my husband!" Clara screamed, pushing between them and trying to shield her battered and broken husband.

"Well, Mrs. Truitt," Longarm said, flexing his hands to see if he'd injured any knuckles. "My advice is to divorce him. He's no damned good. Bullies rarely change except sometimes when they've been taught how it feels to be humiliated and beaten. That's the lesson I've just applied and, for your sake, I hope that it works."

"Mister, you almost killed him!"

"Maybe I saved your life, Mrs. Truitt," Longarm said. "At any rate, it gave me no pleasure to do what needed to be done. I'm sorry about this whole affair."

"I'm not," Billy said, straightening his shirt and coat and gingerly touching a mouse that was going to close his left eye. "Custis, can we order dessert now?"

"Sure," Longarm said, taking his place back at his table as Clara helped her still-sobbing husband out of the room.

It was several minutes before Billy inspected his knuckles and said, "I learned something here, Custis. I'm not nearly the man I was even ten years ago."

"None of us are."

"*You* are."

"Shut up and let's enjoy our dessert," Longarm said without anger.

"You might have saved Mrs. Truitt and her marriage. That man will never be quite the same. You really broke up his face and probably his spirit."

"He was mean to the bone," Longarm said. "I'll bet he's beat plenty of men . . . and women worse than I just beat him. He needed a big dose of humility."

"You gave him that, all right."

Longarm signaled for whiskey. After what had just happened, he thought they could use a drink or two. Quickly, the room was tidied up, and most of the customers even returned to finish their meals. Everyone was staring at Longarm, but he really couldn't imagine why.

When they were finished with dessert and had another drink, Longarm pulled out his pocket watch and said, "It's time for me to collect my bags and get going."

"I wish I were coming along."

"I know, Billy. But maybe you can sort things out here better and keep me up to date on any more deaths of a similar nature should they be brought to your attention."

"That's not too likely, is it?"

"No," Longarm admitted. "It's not. I have another problem you ought to know about."

"What?"

"You know that young lady that I saved from being run over in the street?"

"The one whose dog was shot by the man you killed?"

"The same."

"What about her?"

"She's insisting that she come along."

Billy gaped. "Where?"

"To Reno."

"Well, tell her no!"

"I did. She's coming anyway."

"Shit!" Billy swore. "Isn't there something you can do to stop her?"

"I even tried insulting her. Told her that I would ignore her, but it didn't change her mind."

"Well," Billy said with a sigh. "Then you'll just

have to shake her from your trail once you leave Reno. I shouldn't imagine that would be too hard.''

"I guess not."

"Don't 'guess not' me! Custis, the very last damn thing you need is a lovesick woman trailing you while you're trying to track down the Rebel Executioner."

"I know that, Billy. But Miss Martin is a very stubborn and independently wealthy woman. And, this *is* a free country, as she was quick to remind me. So I don't have any choice but to let her come to Reno."

"Just shake her once you leave there," Billy said. "Damn! You sure don't need any complications on this assignment."

"Don't worry," Longarm vowed, "I'll shake her from my trail. She'll probably get to Reno and decide that she's made a bad mistake and come back on the first train."

"Yeah," Billy said, but he didn't look very happy.

Chapter 4

"All aboard!" the conductor of the Denver Pacific Railroad shouted for the last time. "Final boarding!"

Longarm sat in his very well-appointed first-class compartment with a smile on his lips. Lucy Martin hadn't come to the station to follow him to Reno, and he couldn't have been more pleased. He had her address and would, of course, drop her a line, if time permitted.

Longarm watched as the conductor glanced up and down along the platform and then started to reach down and raise the passengers' step platform. Suddenly, Lucy appeared with her skirts flying. Longarm stared as three strong young men carrying Lucy's baggage came struggling along in her wake. And that wasn't all! Two more burly men, obviously out of breath and straining for all they were worth, came into sight, and they were lugging the biggest damned wooden chest that Longarm had seen in his entire life. And it must have been packed because the pair that were carrying it were really laboring.

Lucy was the first to reach the conductor, and although Longarm couldn't hear their conversation over the sound of the locomotive's engine, it was clear that the conductor was not too pleased by this last-minute complication. But Lucy was waving her ticket in one hand and money in the other. That being the case, Longarm was not surprised when the conductor not only let her come aboard, but took her money and then *helped* load her baggage and heavy wooden chest.

"Damn!" Longarm swore, shaking his head in disgust. "I guess I should have expected she wouldn't give up so easy."

He didn't go out to meet Lucy, but sat brooding in his compartment, waiting for the train to finally pull out of the station on its way up to Cheyenne, where he and the westbound passengers would transfer to the Union Pacific Railroad. Thanks to Lucy, the whole train was about five minutes late getting out of Denver, but you couldn't have told it by the smiling conductor and the smiling hired help that Lucy paid off before she waved them all good-bye.

Longarm picked up the newspaper and read it with scant interest until the train was finally on its way and rolling out of town. About sundown, Longarm heard a knock on his door and then the sweet, familiar voice of Lucy Martin.

"Custis, aren't you going to ask me to dine with you?"

"No. Go away."

"Custis!"

Longarm opened his door, and had intended to say something cross, but then he saw how pretty Lucy was looking, and succumbed both to her beauty and the smell of those roses and wound up asking, "How are you doing?"

"Well," she said, planting a kiss on his cheek. "It has been one hell of an afternoon. Mrs. Harney was absolutely devastated about my leaving. She didn't want to stay alone, so I had to scurry around all over Denver trying to find her a living companion. It's a good thing I am involved in so many charities or I should never have succeeded. Mrs. Harney would have had to join us, Custis."

"Now that would have been something."

"Don't be cynical, dear. Mrs. Harney is a sweetheart and you know that she's an excellent cook."

"Lucy, I'm not going to be in some mansion waiting for dinner every night! I'm going to be out on the trail, sleeping in the dirt, eating when I can but going without plenty often. Don't you have even the vaguest idea of my job?"

"No," Lucy admitted, "so why don't you fill me in on the the dirty little details. I know that you'll make it sound just as wretched as you possibly can."

"It's no place for a lady."

"Of course it's not. But I've already demonstrated that I'm not a lady." Lucy even blushed. "I'm sure you haven't forgotten that."

"No," he said. "But I just don't see why you have to persist in this idea about being my companion on a manhunt. It isn't going to be fun or easy."

"Will you have to kill him?"

"Probably, or he'll kill me."

"I see." Lucy bravely forced a smile. "Then I'm all the more determined to help you, Custis. And look! Bullets!"

She produced a handful of them from her purse and

held them out along with the derringer. "Would you kindly show me how it works?"

"Not now, Lucy. Maybe later."

"Good!" She put the bullets and weapon back in her purse. "I take that to mean that you are at least starting to become accustomed to the idea of my coming with you."

"Then you take it wrong."

"I don't think so," she said with a wink.

"Stop it, Lucy!" he snapped. "This isn't some kind of lark. This is a deadly damned game where a lot of lives have been lost, and if I fail, will *continue* to be lost."

Lucy's smile dissolved, and she gazed out the window at the rolling hills of northeastern Colorado for several minutes before she turned to Longarm and said, "I never thought for a minute that it would be a lark. I'm not naive about you or the work that you do."

"Well, then, why get involved?"

"Because you are the handsomest, most exciting man I have ever met and I owe you my life."

"You don't owe me a thing, Lucy. I'd have done the same for anyone."

"Oh, I know that. But it doesn't change the facts of the matter, does it? And furthermore, I have always believed that I was meant to do something rather special. And by that, I mean rather out of the norm, if you will. Something quite remarkable."

"And you've come to think that going on this manhunt with me is it?"

"That's correct. You see, Custis, I've waited and waited for something to show me what it was that I was supposed to do so remarkably well. I've even prayed about it most nights. But year after year has passed and

I've seen no sign of anything until the very moment that you rushed into that crowded street, killed the beast that shot my Prince, and then saved my life. It was then that I knew you were the one who was meant to take me on the adventure of my life.''

"Lucy, it might *end* your life!"

"That wouldn't matter. You see, I believe we all have our destiny. And the important thing is not how many years we live, but how well we live and how well we fulfill our destiny. Because if we just do that, we have accomplished our purpose for living.''

Longarm rubbed his eyes with his thumb and forefinger. "That all sounds like some religious nonsense that you must have heard shouted over and over in a tent show revival meeting.''

"Stop it!" Lucy lowered her voice. "You have to understand something, Custis. *Nothing* can prevent me from fulfilling my destiny with you on this case. You may think you can outwit and lose me, but you can't. I have almost unlimited funds, and I will hire whomever it takes to track you down and deliver me to your side.''

"No!" Longarm shouted. "That would be the worst possible thing that you could do.''

"Why?"

"Because the only thing I have to my advantage is surprise. Whoever is committing these murders—and it may be several people or even some secret organization—cannot know who I am and what my purpose is. Or else I'll be killed, or they will go to ground and I'll never solve the case.''

"Then you had better not try and skip out on me, Custis. Surely you must understand that. Now, can we go to the dining car? I'm famished.''

Longarm wanted to grab her and shake some sense

into her, but he wasn't a bit certain that would do any good. Frankly, he'd never seen such a determined woman. Maybe she was even a little crazy. He just didn't know. All that he knew for sure was that she was smart, pretty, and committed to getting into something that was way, way over her head. He was also sure that she could be trusted and was completely courageous, even to the point where she would give her own life in order to save his. That was a very sobering realization and one that Longarm could not, in conscience, take lightly.

"Don't be mean or angry with me, Custis. We're in this *together* and I promise you that, when it's over, you'll be very glad that I insisted on coming along."

"I wish that I could believe that, Lucy. I really do. But I'm afraid that you'll get killed and maybe even get me killed. It's just that I don't want to be responsible for your life."

"Then don't be! Hold *me* completely responsible because you have done everything but bite my head off in order to dissuade me from coming along. Now, isn't that true?"

"It sure is."

"So what could you possibly feel guilty about if I am killed trying to help you?"

Longarm gave up the argument right then and there. Lucy was never going to change her mind and listen to reason, and he damn sure could not afford to have her hire someone to track him down and, in the process, expose him.

He was licked. She had won. He was hungry.

"Let's go eat, Lucy."

"Good!" She jumped up and hugged him tightly.

"We'll pull into Cheyenne late this evening and switch trains."

"That's right. Have you made your reservations?"

"No," she said, tipping her head back and gazing up at him. "I mean, yes, I was able to get a ticket, but not a compartment in first class. A third-class seat was the only ticket available. Custis, you won't be mean and make me sleep on a wooden bench all the way to Reno, will you?"

He sighed because there were some pretty rough and ready men who slept and drank whiskey in third class, and a pretty young woman without the protection of a man, especially one as obviously wealthy as Lucy, would be easy prey. She'd be mauled, or at the very least, harassed and humiliated.

"No, dammit. Of course not."

"Thank you!" Lucy cried, tears springing into her eyes. "I *knew* that you'd forgive me and that you were too much the Southern gentleman to throw me to the wolves."

"Come on," Longarm said, opening the door to his compartment and stepping into the narrow corridor that ran down the length of this coach. "Let's go eat and I'll tell you everything I know about the Rebel Executioner."

"*That's* his name?"

"It's just the one that we've given him until we expose his or their true identity."

"But how do you know—"

"Lucy, I'll tell you over dinner, but you have to promise me to keep your voice low because, from this moment on, I'm *not* a United States marshal."

"Then who are you?"

"I haven't decided yet."

"I know," Lucy cried. "You can be my late husband!"

"Not on your life," Longarm said. "I'll come up with something."

"Please make me your wife! Just think of how it solves everything."

"How do you figure?"

"Well," Lucy said, "no one would dream that a federal marshal would be accompanied by his wife."

Longarm almost smiled, but he let it pass as they moved into the dining car. Maybe Lucy was a little crazy, but she damn sure wasn't stupid.

"Marshal Long!" the dining car headwaiter said with a wide grin. "What a pleasure to finally have you join us in first-class dining."

"Uh . . . thanks," Longarm muttered in a low voice as Lucy squeezed his arm and began to giggle.

After dinner, they adjourned to Longarm's compartment, where they talked about the case of the Rebel Executioner. Mostly, Longarm was voicing his own thoughts and feelings concerning the tragic and mysteriously related deaths. He was surprised and quite pleased to discover that Lucy actually could be a very good listener.

"So," he ended up saying, "the connection *must* be the war, and in particular, some specific battles that linked a Confederate soldier-turned-assassin with his victims."

"Yes," Lucy agreed. "Couldn't the State Department, or the War Department—"

"No," Longarm interrupted. "The names of those who survived the major battles are not on record. Furthermore, the names of those who died or disappeared are also unavailable. I am told that the desertion rate was sometimes as high as twenty percent on both sides of the battle lines.''

"That many?"

"Yes," Longarm said. "There were some battles where the carnage was so great that, when the tide turned and one side retreated, it was chaos. After men have been broken in a rout like that, they often can't ever summon the nerve to fight again. I've seen far too many."

"You were in the war?"

"Yes," Longarm said, his eyes becoming distant. "But don't ask me anything about it. I work too hard trying to forget the sights, sounds, and smells of the war and the cries of the wounded and dying."

Lucy touched his hand and then changed the subject. "So you are going to see this woman in the slim hope that she might be able to provide you with more information or even news of some new tragedies."

"That's right. The last newspaper clipping is about four months old. I really need a much fresher trail."

"Well," Lucy replied, "I'm sure that we can come up with some more answers when we arrive in Reno. Maybe my friend even knows some people who can help."

"*That,*" Longarm said with emphasis, "would be exactly the wrong thing to do. I insist on secrecy."

"You mean, like when we went into the dining car?" Lucy asked, giving him an impish smile.

"That will change," he promised. "I ride this railroad line so frequently that I suppose it was stupid to think that I would not be recognized by any of the railroad employees. However, I'm far less well known on the Union Pacific Railroad, and I know only a few people in Reno."

"I see. I still want to be your wife on this adventure."

"Don't call it an adventure, Lucy. Call it a deadly manhunt."

"Very well," Lucy agreed. "How much longer will it take before we get to Cheyenne?"

"Another hour," he replied, extracting his pocket watch. "Give or take fifteen minutes. We were a bit late getting out of Denver."

"Because of me?"

"That's right."

"I'm sorry . . . no, I'm *not* sorry. In fact, I'm glad."

"Why?"

"Because," Lucy said, starting to unbutton her blouse, "we have just about enough time to enjoy ourselves."

Longarm watched as she undressed, and it was a beautiful sight for his tired eyes.

"Your turn, Custis."

He laughed and shucked out of his clothes in no time at all. When he mounted Lucy and let the rocking motion of the train do all the initial lovemaking, Lucy pinched his bare butt and made it plain that she wanted him to get serious.

Longarm didn't mind at all.

Chapter 5

After reaching Cheyenne, they had transferred to the Union Pacific Railroad, and then had spent the next four leisurely days traveling in style. Their train had chugged bravely across the rolling southern plains of Wyoming where antelope were commonplace, then over the dry alkaline reaches of northern Utah past the Great Salt Lake, and finally along the stinking Humboldt River, which was their companion across northern Nevada until they arrived in Reno.

During the entire trip, Longarm and Lucy had done little except to eat, sleep, and make love while living like royalty. It had been, Longarm concluded, the best four days of his life, and it would not have been nearly as enjoyable traveling alone.

"What happens now?" Lucy asked as their train came to a screeching halt at the Reno train depot.

"Well," Longarm replied, "I had thought to take a room at the Frontier Hotel down by the Truckee River.

It's a nice hotel and one that I have always enjoyed. But on reflection, I can see now that it would be far wiser to stay someplace that I'm not known and will not be recognized.''

"What about *us*?"

"Give me the name and address of the friend whose house you will be staying at and I'll come by first chance."

"Uh-uh," Lucy objected. "The friend I mention never replied to my telegram, and besides, we really weren't *that* good of friends."

"Oh, for crying out loud! I thought . . ."

"What can I say?" Lucy shrugged. "And besides, we need to stick right close together, or you might decide you're too busy and try to go off on your own. We'll take up residence at a hotel as man and wife. It's a perfect ruse."

"You think so, huh?"

"Of course! And this way, I'll always keep you practically in sight."

"All right," Longarm agreed, realizing that he really didn't want to say good-bye to Lucy after the wonderful time they'd been having. "But when I go out to start tracking down some answers, I'd prefer to work alone. I always have and that's the way I operate best."

"Very well, just as long as you return to our room each evening and take me out to dinner and then to bed."

He blushed. "That's a deal I won't refuse."

So they left the train and found an exceptionally nice two-story hotel on South Virginia Street. It was relatively new and catered to a wealthy clientele. A porter took their bags and carried them to the registration desk. Lucy's large wooden chest and some of her other luggage had been left at the depot for the time being.

"Welcome to the Truckee House," the porter said, beaming from ear to ear. "We are delighted to have you as our guests."

Longarm studied the elegant mahogany woodwork, much of it hand-carved, the deep, plush carpets, and the massive chandeliers that hung over the lobby. Original oil paintings graced the walls, and the few people he saw in the lobby were extremely well dressed.

"It's good to be here," he said, taking up a silver pen and then signing himself and Lucy in as Mr. and Mrs. Custis Long from Cheyenne.

"A rancher, I'll bet," the hotel clerk behind the expansive counter said with a big grin.

"That's right," Longarm replied, wishing he had thought to dress a little more the part. His own suit and clothes, while clean and nice, were neither expensive nor impressive. "I'm a cattle rancher."

"Excellent! Welcome to our new hotel, which is the finest in Nevada. May I inquire as to how long will you be staying as our guests?"

"I have no idea. It all depends on how long I need to settle my business matters."

"Of course. A day or a month or a year. Whatever time we can serve as your hosts will be our pleasure, Mr. and Mrs. Long! Now, I will have Murphy take you and your baggage up to your rooms. We'll have fresh flowers and a bucket of iced champagne sent up immediately."

Longarm was impressed, but also a little concerned about what all this was going to cost. After all, he was using the money of taxpayers, and he certainly didn't want to stiff them, even though he had spent hundreds of nights in dirty little hovels across the West saving them money.

"What is my room rate?" he asked.

The man looked disappointed, as if Longarm shouldn't really have asked. He cleared his throat, then said, "It is thirty-three dollars a night . . . but the champagne, service, and of course the flowers are all complimentary."

"Fine," Longarm said, knowing that he could not back out now. It would look pretty ridiculous, and would certainly destroy his new identity.

They were escorted up to the room, and Longarm tipped Murphy the porter. Before Lucy could even get her dress off, there was a firm knock at the door, and the bellman brought in a gorgeous bouquet of flowers and a silver tray with champagne on ice. Longarm tipped the man and then closed the door.

"Whew!" he said. "This place is *really* expensive. Billy is just going to have a fit when he finally gets the tab."

"By then," Lucy said, glancing over at the handsome hotel bed with its beautiful satin spread, "we'll have arrested the Rebel Executioner and you'll be a national celebrity. Now, why don't we enjoy ourselves for a while?"

Longarm was bothered by the fact that he could not tell Lucy that his orders were to *kill* whomever it was behind the deaths. And while he would have enjoyed spending some time drinking the iced champagne, he'd spent so much money already that he was feeling too guilty.

"I'm going out to meet my boss's cousin. Her name is Carole Shaw."

"I know. You already told me all about her sending

62

those articles. Custis, I know that I promised I'd stay here and wait, but I'd really like to go with you and meet this woman.''

''I'd prefer that you didn't,'' Longarm said. ''I'll be back by this evening and we'll go to dinner.''

''All right,'' Lucy said, looking disappointed. ''But if you don't return by eight o'clock, I'll come looking for you, and believe me, it won't be all that difficult to find where Miss Shaw lives.''

''I'll be back by then. Just sit tight.''

''I'll find something to occupy myself with. Reno looks like a pleasant town.''

''It can be that,'' Longarm said, thinking of all the good times he'd had here.

Longarm kissed Lucy good-bye and then headed downstairs and over to the registration desk. ''How many daily newspapers are there in this town?''

''Two,'' the registration clerk answered. ''And we carry them both for sale right here in the lobby.''

''Good. I'll have a copy of each.''

Longarm paid for the papers, and then sat down in one of the plush velvet chairs that were perfectly arranged in the lobby. For the next fifteen minutes, he scanned the newspapers. Sure enough, one of them had an article by Carole Shaw, and he already knew the location of her office.

Fifteen minutes later, he was striding into the office of the *Reno Daily News* and asking for Miss Carole Shaw. Because Billy Vail was short and on the heavy side, Longarm was expecting a short, rather dumpy woman with hands stained by newsprint, but was greeted by a tall, willowy woman with silver in her hair and sharp, penetrating brown eyes that looked very large behind her wire-rimmed spectacles.

"I'm Miss Carole Shaw. How can I help you?" the woman asked after giving Longarm a very firm, very businesslike handshake before folding her arms across her chest and regarding him in thoughtful silence.

"Miss Shaw, I have something I need to speak to you about in private."

"Concerning?"

"Newspaper articles and obituaries you sent to the man I work for . . . Marshal Billy Vail. Here is a letter he wrote to you," he said, handing her Billy's letter.

The woman didn't bat an eye, but nodded her chin almost imperceptibly and said, "Come into my office, Mr. . . ."

"Long. Custis Long. I'm now a successful Wyoming cattle rancher."

"I see. Follow me, please."

Carole's office was a bit less spartan than the other offices which Longarm passed and peered into. She had added curtains to the windows, but not the lacy kind. There were also etchings and paintings on the walls, and several plaques which Longarm did not have time to read, but which he was sure were awards won by Miss Shaw in her newspaper work.

Ten years ago, it would have been extremely rare to have found a woman reporter or editor, but that was changing, and some women were proving themselves more than capable as reporters, columnists, and editors.

"Please sit down," Carole said, indicating a chair a moment before she closed the door so that they could talk in private. After scanning Billy's letter, she looked up. "Your timing couldn't have been better, Mr. Long. We just finished up on tomorrow's paper and it has gone into production. That means that I can spend some time with you on this . . . very sad matter."

"Good."

"But first, how is dear Billy? His letter is somewhat vague."

"He's a little beat up right now, but he'll be fine."

"Beat up?"

Longarm quickly explained how Billy had lost his temper and jumped in to help a woman named Clara, and had gotten whipped for his good intentions.

"And you let him get whipped by a far younger and stronger man?"

"I stepped in the moment he asked me," Longarm said without recounting the outcome of the fight. "He'd have been insulted if I'd come to his aid any sooner."

"Better insulted than damaged by some brute!"

"I assure you," Longarm said, "he isn't 'damaged.' Far from it. In fact, he is one of the most capable men I've ever worked with."

"Let's hope that doesn't change because of fighting."

"It won't, Miss Shaw. Billy just gets a little crazy once in a while. I think he misses the excitement of working in the field. Right now, he'd rather be on this case than doing anything else in the world."

"Is that so?"

"Yes. Definitely."

Carole Shaw relaxed. She surprised Longarm by reaching into her desk and selecting a very thin, very black cigar. "Would you like one?"

"No, thanks," Longarm replied as Carole lit up her smoke and inhaled deeply. When she began to speak, smoke trailed lazily out her nostrils. Longarm liked that. He liked the way that this woman shook his hand and handled herself. Very professional and very straightforward. She was the kind of a woman who didn't beat around the bush and got right down to cases.

"You know, Marshal Long . . ."

"*Mr.* Long, remember?"

"I'm sorry. All right. Mr. Long. Anyway, I was about to tell you that Billy was always the sweet protective one. That's why I shouldn't have been so shocked when you told me he jumped in to protect that woman from her bullying husband. The surprising thing is that Billy was never especially big or strong, but right from the start he possessed the very heart of a lion."

"He still does," Longarm said with a smile. "I couldn't ask for a better boss."

"Well," Carole said, sitting in her desk. "He must think a great deal of you, or he wouldn't have chosen you among so many others to come out here and put an end to this business."

"Have you any *later* incidents to bring to my attention? It would help a lot to investigate more recent deaths."

"Yes, I do," Carole said, reaching into her desk and pulling out a manila file folder. "Two more. One that took place exactly fifteen days ago right here in Reno. The other happened about eight weeks ago. I clipped the account from a newspaper called the *Territorial Enterprise* which is published in Virginia City on the Comstock Lode."

"Mark Twain worked for it, didn't he?"

"That's right! He was brilliant, but I prefer the style and reporting of Dan De Quille, another old-time reporter and the one who wrote this article."

"I've met Dan a time or two," Longarm said. "He's one of the best I've ever seen."

"I couldn't agree more. I read everything he writes, and that's how I happened to come across this article that I'm going to give you. You see, Mr. Long, like Dan

De Quille, I have been in this newspaper business long enough to smell out things that don't quite ring true.''

"I'm sure you have, Miss Shaw."

"Carole. Let's proceed on a first-name basis."

"Fine."

"Anyway," Carole said, smoking faster, "I believe that these two new cases involving Union heroes have far too many similarities with the other cases to be unrelated."

"Well," Longarm said, "they will at least provide me a fresher trail."

"I think there may be more than one murderer doing this," Carole suggested.

"What gives you that impression?"

"I don't exactly know," she said with a shrug. "There's something in these last two accounts that smacks of a group. A fanatic group of revenge-seekers working in tandem. I'll give you these articles and you tell me what you think."

"I will," Longarm promised.

Carole studied him. "Where are you staying right now?"

"The Truckee House."

"My heavens! I never realized that government people had it so good!"

"We don't," Longarm replied defensively. "But Billy and everyone above him felt that this case demanded extraordinary efforts, and I've practically been given access to the United States Mint in order to get it solved as quickly and quietly as possible."

"What do you mean, quietly?"

"It's just that the President doesn't want—"

"The President of the United States!" For the first time, Longarm saw through Carole's cool and professional veneer as she blinked and then stared at him with disbelief.

"Yes," Longarm said. "This matter was thought to be so politically sensitive that even the President was consulted. He's worried about renewing old hatreds in the South. The last thing that he wants, or this country needs, is to resurrect the Confederacy behind some murdering lunatic or lunatics."

"I understand what you mean," Carole said. "But I was hoping that this would become the biggest story of my career. The one that would make my name and send me to a plush job in San Francisco."

"I'm sorry to disappoint you."

"Ah, well," Carole said with a shrug, "that's all right. I like living here in Reno a lot, and I do have a nice boyfriend."

"Good for you," Longarm said. "I'm traveling with a lady friend."

"Really?"

"Yes," Longarm said, offering a half-truth. "I decided that having a 'wife' would further diminish any suspicions."

"What a convenient line of thinking," Carole said with dry humor. "And I suppose that she's also staying at the Truckee House?"

"Where else?"

"Yes, where else."

Longarm was desperate to read the two new accounts, but Carole insisted that he do so elsewhere and then meet her after work at the Virginia Street Bridge, which spanned the Truckee River.

"We can stroll along the parkway as long as we wish and examine our separate theories," Carole said, escorting him to the door of her office.

"At five?"

"Five after five would be better," Carole said. "And please don't be late."

"I won't," Longarm promised.

Longarm took the two articles and went to the park, where he read them each twice. One was about a Captain Lester Gorton who had fought at Gettysburg and led an especially gallant charge through the Confederate lines thwarting a major offensive. It seemed that Gorton's cavalry charge had also rescued several high-ranking Union officers. Most of Gorton's cavalry had been either killed or wounded, and those that had survived had all been given medals.

Gorton had retired a year later as one of the most heavily decorated soldiers in the Union Army. Unlike some of the other men involved in this case, Lester Gorton had pretty much become a failure. He'd failed at farming corn in Nebraska, sheep ranching in Colorado, and silver mining in Nevada. He'd failed at being a saloon owner in Austin, Nevada, and had wound up being a part-time bartender in Reno.

Lester Gorton, down on his luck and with failing health, might have lived a few more years in frustrated obscurity if someone hadn't discovered that he was a recipient of the Medal of Honor and that his old Union Army uniform was one of the most decorated in United States history.

Apparently, Gorton had been revitalized by his sudden celebrity. With a gift of oratory, he'd given dozens of speeches about national unity and indivisibility and charged his listeners one dollar each. It was said that there was never a dry eye in the audience when Captain Gorton began to tell the stories of his gallantry and that of his cavalry. He also spoke of President Abe Lincoln and about the wisdom and sacrifice necessary to preserve the Union. Shortly after one of his most passionate speeches at the town hall, Lester Gorton had died of what was described as a "self-inflicted mortal wound to the temple."

A Dr. Ronald Maxwell who'd examined his body had determined that poor old Lester Gorton, after one of his greatest performances ever, had become extremely over-wrought and must have lost his sanity. Using his own gun, Gorton had put a bullet into his brain without bothering to say good-bye to anyone or to leave a suicide note.

Longarm could find nothing in the article about Lester Gorton having a family, and supposed that the Civil War hero had been a lifelong bachelor. That was good in the sense that he had left no close and grieving family members, but bad in that it offered few leads that would provide better insight into Gorton's real state of mind. Therefore, Longarm decided that the best place to find out more about Lester Gorton, the war hero, was to visit the saloon where he'd worked, and perhaps the doctor who had pronounced him dead and whose name was written up in the lengthy and laudatory obituary.

The second case given to him by Carole Shaw was far more tragic and involved another entire family, this one living in Virginia City. Longarm would have to go up there and talk to Dan De Quille and whomever else he could find in order to create a background and any possible leads.

At precisely five minutes after five o'clock, Longarm met Carole Shaw beside the Truckee River. After a quick greeting, they began to walk along the river and discuss the Gorton "suicide."

"I hope," Carole began, "that you didn't think it really *was* a suicide."

"No," Longarm replied, "I did not. But then, men who seem to be happy one minute have been known to blow their brains out the very next."

"That's true."

"Was Lester Gorton a drunk?"

"No. He was a heavy drinker, but I'm quite sure that he was not a drunk. If he had been, he would never have been able to hold down a job tending bar."

"Good point," Longarm agreed. "No family?"

"Gorton was married for a short period, but divorced many years ago. He had no children, but a lot of casual friends. Everyone liked and admired him, especially after he became such a celebrity. I interviewed someone named Pete Black who was apparently Gorton's best friend. Black swears that Gorton would never have blown his brains out."

"Did Black have any idea who might have done it?"

"No," Carole said. "Black says that Lester Gorton didn't have an enemy in the world. He was, however, in debt to several merchants and was always broke."

"How much in debt?"

"Not much," Carole replied. "Only a hundred dollars or two. Certainly not enough to the kill the man for. I couldn't pursue the matter any further because it is not the kind of thing a newspaper reporter is supposed to include in a local hero's obituary."

"Of course it isn't," Longarm said. "But we haven't much information to work with."

"Pete Black is a genuine drunk and he'll bend your ear pretty hard," Carole warned, "but he's a good, honest man and it was clear that he was devastated by Gorton's death. He might be able to help you. I'm sure that he will if he can. I'd talk to him and some of Gorton's other close friends.''

"What's the name of the saloon where Gorton tended bar?''

"It's called the Aces High.''

"I know the place,'' Longarm said. "Where does Dr. Maxwell have his office?''

"Just up the street two blocks. He might still be working.''

"I think that's where I should start,'' Longarm said, "and I think that I will start right now.''

"I'll come along and introduce you if he's still there,'' Carole offered.

"It might be best if you didn't.''

"What are you going to tell him when he asks what your relationship to Gorton was?''

It was a question that Longarm had been considering for days, and he still didn't have a very good answer. "I'll just tell him that Gorton had some inheritance money coming and that I am the executor of the estate.''

"Do you really think Dr. Maxwell will fall for something like that?''

"He will if he believes he's owed some money from Lester Gorton for his services, no matter how small the amount. And when I offer to pay him that money, I am sure that he'll be willing to answer my questions.''

"Yes,'' Carole said, "I believe you are right. That's a very clever ruse.''

"I don't know how clever it is,'' Longarm confessed, "but I do have one hell of a big expense account that makes it possible. Besides, like you, I can usually sort out the truth from the lies. If Dr. Maxwell knows *anything* unusual about Lester Gorton's death, I'll find it out from him.''

"Are you sure that you don't want me to come along for the introduction?"

"Oh, why not?" Longarm said, changing his mind. "I can't really see how it could hurt. I'll just explain that we are old friends."

"I am beginning to wish that we were," Carole said, "especially if I were about twenty years younger and didn't have such a nice boyfriend."

"Oh, well," Longarm said, flattered by that comment, as they started walking up Virginia Street toward the bridge.

Chapter 6

As it turned out, Longarm and Carole got lucky. Dr. Ronald Maxwell was still in his office, just preparing to leave. After Longarm was introduced by Carole as the "executor" of an estate with an inheritance left to Lester Gorton, Dr. Maxwell suddenly became quite cordial.

"You know, I *am* due some fees for my services," he said. "Not only for attending the poor man's death, but also because I was his personal physician and he owed me a fair amount of money. Lester Gorton was a courageous man, but he was not a healthy one. I supplied him with medications and the best medical care that I could provide."

"How much money did he owe you?" Longarm asked in his most solicitous manner.

"I can tell you without even consulting his file, which is locked in the basement of my house. Let's see, Lester Gorton owed me . . . yes, eighty-nine dollars and fifty cents. That's the exact figure, Mr. . . . ."

"Long."

"Yes of course. I . . . I don't suppose that you have this inheritance money in your possession and could disperse it to Mr. Gorton's creditors . . . starting with me."

"As a matter of fact, I am having it sent to me from . . . from Nebraska, where his family still has its roots. It should arrive and I'll be able to reimburse you very soon."

"That's wonderful!" Dr. Maxwell exclaimed. "Things have been a little lean lately. And I'm sure that Mr. Gorton would have considered me his favorite creditor."

"No doubt about that," Longarm said. "Do you mind if I ask you some *other* personal questions about Lester Gorton? There may be other creditors and some family that none of us know about."

Judging from his frail appearance, Maxwell was not a well man himself. He looked to be in his early sixties, with dark circles under sunken eyes. He was balding and very thin. He had a narrow face and a hawk-shaped nose laced with red and blue capillaries. Great dark veins ribbed the backs of his hands, and his fingernails were bloodless, evidence of a man with poor circulation to his extremities.

"I don't think that Mr. Gorton had any family whatsoever," Maxwell offered after a moment of consideration. "At least, he never spoke of any to me and he was a very talkative man."

"You wrote on his death certificate that the cause of death was suicide."

"That's correct. It's really quite common. More so up on the Comstock Lode, where you have a lot of foreign miners who despair of ever returning to their native

76

countries with the wealth that they'd looked forward to.''

"But I understand that on Gorton's last night, he had just given an excellent and well-received lecture on his role in the Civil War.''

"So I've heard,'' Maxwell agreed.

"And that he spoke to a big, *paying* audience, Dr. Maxwell. That means he must have earned a very healthy fee for his speech and should have been in high spirits.''

"Too high,'' Maxwell said. "My guess is that he got to celebrating and became dead drunk. That's why he shot himself to death.''

"Because he was celebrating?'' Carole asked with raised eyebrows. "That doesn't make sense.''

"*Nothing* about suicide ever does,'' Maxwell offered with a sad shake of his head. "It happens to the rich, to the poor, to those of us in the middle. It happens to people with big problems and little problems. Healthy or sick. You figure it out, because I can't.''

Longarm believed Dr. Maxwell. So, apparently, did Carole Shaw. That being the case, they asked a few more questions, and then Longarm excused himself by saying, "Well, Doctor, thank you for your time.''

"My pleasure, Mr. Long. My pleasure. I really liked Lester. He was a certified war hero. I knew that right from the beginning, you see.''

"He told you?''

"No. The first time that I examined him I saw all the old war wounds and questioned him about them. Initially, he was almost embarrassed to talk about his heroics, but that eventually changed when he realized that we all love heroes. And Lester Gorton, make no mistake about it, was a true and genuine American hero.''

"Not if you were or still are a Southern sympathizer, or can't forgive the North for what it did and still is doing to the defeated South," Carole said.

Maxwell blinked with confusion. "I . . . I don't understand your meaning, Miss Shaw."

"What about those who *hate* the victorious North and revile anyone who fought for the Union Army? Don't tell me that you haven't seen and heard them."

"Of course I have, though not so much as I used to."

"That's only because they have just managed to bury their animosities," Carole argued. "There are still plenty of men who would take up arms for the Confederacy if ever it was to rise."

"Why are you saying this?"

"She was wondering," Longarm interjected, "if you might have considered the fact that Lester Gorton was murdered by someone who became incensed at his patriotism and love of the Union and of Abraham Lincoln."

"Most certainly not!"

"Why not?" Longarm asked. "Why is it so hard for you to imagine a Confederate killer?"

"After all these years? Out here in the West? Why . . . why it just seems so preposterous!"

"It's not," Longarm said.

Dr. Maxwell considered this for a moment, and then he said, "Why is this cause of death such an issue with you, Mr. Long?"

"Why wouldn't it be," he replied evasively. "I'm simply curious, that's all. And so too are Mr. Gorton's grieving relatives."

"Does the disbursement of the inheritance have anything to do with the cause of death?"

Longarm started to say no, then changed his mind.

"That's something that I'm not free to reveal."

"Ah-ha! So, there *is* something in the will about suicide! Was Mr. Gorton's family perhaps of the Roman Catholic faith that considers suicide a grievous mortal sin—one punishable by everlasting damnation?"

"You are very shrewd, Dr. Maxwell. Very, very shrewd. But remember, I said nothing about that."

"Oh, of course! And anyway, I *could* be mistaken about the cause of death. It *might* indeed have been murder. I mean, if the relatives and the estate prohibits. . . ."

"I'm afraid that I am forbidden to discuss this matter any further," Longarm said discreetly. "But if you remember something or in some way come up with evidence that might suggest that Lester Gorton did not commit suicide and was in fact murdered, then it would be very, very comforting to the family and extremely helpful in the settlement of the estate and the affairs of his creditors, you being the first and foremost who would receive satisfaction."

"Yes," Dr. Maxwell said, giving the matter the full power of his concentration. "I see now that I might have been a little hasty doing that examination of Lester's body. However, there is no doubt in my mind whatsoever that the cause of death was due to cerebral hemorrhaging brought about by a bullet."

"Do you have Gorton's gun?"

"No."

"Who does?"

"Marshal Tom Oatman, I guess."

"What kind of weapon was it?"

"A .45-caliber pistol."

"Did you remove the bullet from Gorton's head?"

"I saw no reason to do so. Why? Do you think that

the bullet in Mr. Gorton's head might be something other than a .45?''

''It's possible. What would you charge to exhume the body and extract the bullet?''

''Oh,'' the doctor said, shaking his head back and forth, ''that would be a *very* unpleasant job.''

''I know. How much money will it take to get you to do it?''

''A lot. But remember, the spent slug would be completely misshapen upon impact with the cranium. I know because I have fished lead slugs out of craniums before.''

''Then you also know that the slug could be weighed and its caliber determined if no large fragments had detached upon entry.''

''Yes, that's true,'' Dr. Maxwell admitted. ''But it would be a *grisly* task. A terrible task! One that I'd—''

''The family very, very much wants to know if Lester Gorton took his own life,'' Longarm explained. ''I'm sure they would be willing to pay you . . . oh, a hundred dollars for this unpleasantness.''

Dr. Maxwell gulped, and actually appeared unwell at the prospect, but Longarm knew that he had correctly judged the man's desperate financial circumstances when the physician dipped his pointed chin.

''All right. But I insist on being paid in advance, and that I keep the money even if I cannot retrieve the slug.''

''No,'' Longarm said, ''fifty dollars now, fifty more when I have the slug—all of it—in my possession, along with its exact weight and comparison with a .45-caliber slug.''

''You are a hard, hard bargainer.''

''Doctor,'' Carole said, injecting herself into the con-

80

versation, "I believe that Mr. Long has little choice in this sad and confusing affair."

"That's true," Longarm agreed.

"Very well, then," the physician said. "Give me the fifty dollars. And, oh, I'll need another twenty to hire a grave digger both to exhume the body and to return it to its final resting place. As you have probably noticed, I am not in any physical condition to do so myself."

"Of course. Sixty now. Sixty when you have completed the task."

Maxwell looked beaten as he stuck out his hand. Longarm wondered if the doctor would open poor Lester's skull right at the side of his empty grave because he would not be able to bring the body into town. However, after a few seconds of consideration, Longarm decided that he really did not want to know anyway.

"You are amazing," Carole Shaw said after Longarm had paid the doctor sixty dollars and they had left his office. "I can't believe what I've just witnessed."

"Why not?"

"Because the entire conversation was so . . . so macabre! So . . . gruesome!"

"And yet so necessary," Longarm said, not feeling a bit offended. "If the bullet that is extracted from Lester Gorton's brain is *not* from a .45-caliber weapon, then we have proof that he was murdered."

"But we're already quite sure of that."

"Yes, but the bullet might be of an unusual caliber, and that would help, wouldn't it?"

"I suppose."

"Trust me, it would," Longarm assured her. "Oh, here is my hotel."

"And your 'wife' is no doubt getting impatient for your arrival."

"No doubt," Longarm replied. "Good evening, Carole."

"Are you going to bed now?" She blushed. Clearing her throat, she restated her question. "I mean, are you going to do anything more about the investigation tonight?"

"I'm going to see if I can find Pete Black and have a few words with him. I guess he's most likely to be found at the Aces High Saloon where Gorton was bartending."

"That would be a good place to start looking," Carole agreed.

With that, Longarm went up to his room and knocked on the door. Without even asking who was there, Lucy swung the door open, then threw herself into his arms. "Where have you been! I was getting very worried!"

"Sit down and I'll tell you all about it," he said, kissing her cheek as he extracted himself from her arms.

Ten minutes later, Longarm had finished recounting his story. "And so, Lucy, that's all I've been up to."

"That's a lot!"

"After dinner I intend to go find Pete Black and see what information I can pry out of him regarding Lester Gorton's state of mind preceding his death. I also want to make sure that Dr. Maxwell was correct in stating that Gorton's pistol was a .45-caliber."

"Can I go with you?"

"Of course not. The Aces High Saloon will be filled with men, and if you were with me, I'd spend all my time beating them off you instead of getting to interview Pete Black."

"You are having *all* the fun!"

"It's not fun," Longarm assured her. "And you can

bet that Dr. Maxwell isn't going to be having much fun tomorrow morning either.''

Longarm took Lucy to a nice steak house, and then they returned to their hotel room and made passionate love for nearly an hour. By the time that he left to find Pete Black, it was nearly eleven o'clock and downtown Reno was filled with men of every size and description, all boisterous and happily drifting from one saloon to another.

When Longarm stepped into the Aces High, he took its measure in a single, sweeping glance. The saloon was as ordinary as tree bark, with the usual long bar backed by rows of bottles and a mirror. There were the expected card tables in the back of the room, and plenty of other smaller tables where men were sitting and drinking. The saloon had a plank floor that creaked as Longarm crossed over to the bartender.

''I'll have a whiskey,'' Longarm ordered. ''Your best.''

''My best ain't much, mister. It's called Old Twister, and that means that it will twist your guts up like a wet bar rag. If I were you, I'd have a shot of tequila. It's a whole lot better.''

''I'll have a beer,'' Longarm decided.

Longarm waited until he had been served and paid for his beer before he said, ''I'm looking for Pete Black. Is he around tonight?''

''That's him over there with some friends. He's the little guy with the big laugh. Blue flannel shirt, red suspenders. Take a brew over to him and he'll talk nice to you. Take a bottle of rye over to him and he'll be your friend for the rest of his life . . . which probably isn't all that long.''

''He sick?''

"Yeah," the bartender said. "You could put it that way."

"Give me a bottle of rye for Pete," Longarm said, putting down his money.

When he tapped Pete Black on the shoulder and the man turned and stared at him, Longarm knew that he'd made a mistake in buying Pete a full bottle. What the man really needed was coffee, and plenty of it. But maybe, Longarm thought, he was still sober enough to be of some help.

"Pete, my name is Custis Long. Can I buy you a drink?"

"Why, hell, yes!" Pete shouted. "And you can buy all my friends one too!"

Longarm filled every empty glass on the table, and it was amazing how many kept emptying again until his entire bottle was gone.

"Pete," he said, grabbing the little fella under the arms and lifting him out of his chair, "we need to talk."

"More rye whiskey!"

"No," Longarm said, signaling for two beers as he half carried, half dragged Pete over to another table where they could talk alone.

"Who *are* you?" Pete asked, trying to focus.

Longarm went through the same spiel that he'd already given to Dr. Maxwell, only in a much abbreviated form. He had to explain it twice, though, because Pete wasn't much more attentive than a pet rabbit.

"So what I need to know, and you need to think about a minute before answering, is what caliber of gun did Lester use?"

"He only had one gun and that was a .36-caliber Navy Colt."

"Are you sure?"

"Course I'm sure."

"Dr. Maxwell said. . . ."

"Dr. Maxwell is a liar!"

"Hold your voice down," Longarm ordered. "Are you *dead* sure that Lester only had the one .36-caliber?"

"You bet I am!" Pete said, his face stiffening with outrage. "And he didn't kill hisself! Hell, why should he? Lester weren't no gawddamn coward that would choose that way out. Mister, he was murdered, and I told that to everyone who would listen. Trouble was, no gawddamn body would listen, and they just brushed murder aside and called it suicide."

"I'll listen. But not here and not tonight. Do you have a job?"

Pete straightened up in his chair and threw back his narrow shoulders. "Damn right!"

"Good. Where?"

Pete deflated, and struggled to come up with an answer. "Well, sir, I work wherever I *find* work."

"Meet me out in front of this saloon at nine o'clock tomorrow morning. If you're sober, I'll take you to breakfast, and then I'll pay you ten dollars to do the easiest work you ever were paid for."

"What would that be?"

"To talk."

"To talk?"

"That's right," Longarm said. "You talk about Lester and I'll listen. That's the deal."

"Are you serious?"

"Never more than now," Longarm said.

"Let me see the color of your money."

Longarm showed him an impressive roll of bills, and then he toasted Pete Black with a beer and waited until the man had emptied his own glass. Taking out his pocket watch, Longarm said, "It's a few minutes after midnight, Pete. Time for us to get some sleep."

"What . . ."

"Here," Longarm said, giving Pete five dollars. "Get yourself a safe room and a bath and get some sleep. If you spend it on more liquor, I'll wring your skinny neck in the morning. Do you believe me?"

"Gawdamn right I do," Pete said, swaying to his feet and letting Longarm show him out the door.

Chapter 7

True to his word, Pete Black was waiting *outside* the Aces High Saloon at nine o'clock the next morning looking hungover, but acting sober.

"I feel like hell," he growled. "I ain't sure that this talking business is as easy as I expected it to be."

"Let's get some food in your belly and you'll feel a whole lot better," Longarm suggested, taking the man a couple of doors down the street to a cafe.

Longarm ordered black coffee first, lots of it, and then he ordered them both a big breakfast of flapjacks, bacon, toast, and fried eggs.

"I ain't seen this much food on my plate since I was a farm boy," Pete said, digging into his meal with surprising gusto. "Man, oh, man, this is good!"

"If you drank a little less and worked a little more, you could have a big breakfast like this every morning and a bath every night."

"I don't want no bath every night," Pete said, his

cheeks bulging like those of a chipmunk. "And as for the drinkin', well I sure hope you're no preacher. I just can't stomach someone telling me I shouldn't drink so much."

Longarm was enjoying his own breakfast. "All right, Pete, no temperance lectures. I'm not a hypocrite."

"Good!"

"Now," Longarm began, "last night you told me that Lester owned a .36-caliber Navy Colt."

"That's right and I'll tell you the same damned thing this morning."

"You also told me that Lester was murdered. Who do you think did it?"

"Some hate-filled Rebel sonofabitch that still thinks he's carrying on his own private Civil War."

"I happen to agree, except that there may be more than one killer."

"You mean a whole company of them Southern son-ofabitches?"

"Keep your voice down," Longarm cautioned when heads began to turn. "I am trying to get to the bottom of this business, and I'll never do it if you tell half of Reno what I'm up to."

"Who the hell did you say you were?"

"I'm an executor of an estate that wants to know exactly how Lester died."

"What are you talkin' about?"

"Never mind," Longarm said. "I'm paying you to answer *my* questions, not the other way around."

"What else you want to know about my dead friend?" Pete asked, digging into his pancakes. "You ask the questions and I'll try to answer 'em just as long as you're paying."

"That's the spirit," Longarm said. "Did Lester ever talk to you about the Civil War?"

"Sure. Plenty of times."

"Did he ever mention seeing anyone here in Reno that he remembered from that war?"

"Union or Confederate?"

"Confederate."

"No," Pete said. "He met a few Union Army buddies, but never a Confederate that he cared to talk to. You see, Lester still hated the Johnny Rebs. He was always in a lot of pain from old battlefield wounds. He had real bad headaches, and would sometimes wake up screaming with nightmares as he fought them battles over and over in his sleep."

"I'm sorry to hear that."

"And Lester carried enough Rebel lead in his body so that if you collected it all in one lump, it'd make a fair-sized cannon ball."

"Is that a fact?"

"It damn sure is."

"Did he correspond with any old Civil War friends?"

"Nope."

"Did he have any relatives?"

"Yeah, but they all died or stayed back East."

"Did he go to any Civil War reunions?"

"They have them kind of things?"

"They do," Longarm assured the man.

"Why would anyone want to do anything to remind himself of what happened during that bloody damn war?"

"I don't know," Longarm confessed, "but some do. Tell me this, did Lester know a family that lived up in Virginia City? Their last name was Wallace. Mr. and Mrs. Wade Wallace."

"Why, yes," Pete said, "he knew that family quite well. Wade was a fellow officer in the war and I guess they'd gone through hell together."

Longarm dropped his fork to clatter against his plate. "Are you sure?"

"Of course I am. Lester and Wade were longtime friends. I think that they both came from the same part of Nebraska. They were once farm boys. Like me. But Wade Wallace, he was the only one of us that really did good."

"What do you mean?"

"He made money! I mean a lot of damned money. He struck it rich on the Comstock and then went to buyin' mining stocks. Bought 'em low and sold 'em high. He became a pretty important fella."

"Did you know that the entire Wallace family died in a fire?"

Lester paled and his jaw dropped. "No!"

"It's the truth," Longarm said. "A tragic accident."

"They was burned up? The hull danged family!"

"Actually, one survived. She is a fourteen-year-old girl who was staying overnight with a friend. But Mr. and Mrs. Wallace, along with their two boys, all died in the fire."

Pete's eyes filled with tears. He wiped them with his sleeve and shook his head at his plate. "I wish you wouldn't have ever told me that. I surely do. I can't eat no more. I just want to get drunk."

"I'm sorry I made you upset," Longarm said, meaning it. "But I had to ask. You see, I think that there is something really sinister going on, and I'm trying to get to the bottom of it before more innocent people are murdered."

"Are you a Pinkerton?"

"No."

"Then you got to be a federal officer or something like that."

Longarm reached across the table and gripped Pete's thin arm. "Pete," he said, "what I am isn't important. The important thing is that you don't tell *anyone* that I've been asking questions. If they find out that someone is doing that, all our lives could be in danger."

"Really?" Pete sat bolt upright in his chair and glanced from side to side. "Why?"

"Trust me that I know what I'm doing. That's as much as I can tell you."

"You still going to pay me?"

"Of course," Longarm said, handing him ten dollars. "But you *can't* get drunk and start talking about any of this. *Your* life as well as my own could be in danger."

"Okay," Pete said, shaking his head with dejection. "I just feel like gettin' real drunk, though, knowing that the Wallace family was all burned up. I met that family three, maybe four times, and they was real nice considering how much money they had. Treated me like an equal. And now you're saying that the same sonofabitch that shot Lester in the head might have set them on fire?"

"I didn't say that."

"You didn't have to, Mr. Long. I ain't bright, but I ain't *that* stupid."

"Of course you're not. Just be quiet about all of this and let me do my job."

"You could get killed up on the Comstock. Them's mighty clannish folks up there, and they don't like people askin' a lot of questions."

"I know Dan De Quille, and I need to talk to him because he is the one that wrote the obituary. It was easy to tell that he also thought a great deal of the Wallace family. I'm sure he'll be of some help."

"I met Dan once, and his old friend Mark Twain. Of course, Twain went on to bigger and better things. I heard he's changed, and not for the better. But old Dan, he'll never leave the Comstock and he'll never change."

"I expect that's true," Longarm said, handing the owner of the cafe a twenty-dollar bill and saying, "Feed Pete until this money is gone. Food, not drink. Is that clear?"

"Why, sure!" the man said. "I like Pete too."

"Good."

Longarm downed his coffee and left some of his own breakfast on the plate. He thought that he might just go up to the Comstock Lode today and talk to Dan De Quille. By tomorrow, Dr. Maxwell ought to have gotten him the answers he needed concerning that bullet that he extracted from Lester's cranium. And the fact that Maxwell claimed he'd found a .45-caliber pistol in Lester's lifeless fist sure didn't add up to the story he'd just heard from Pete. No, sir, it didn't add up at all.

Longarm returned to his hotel, and was surprised to see that Carole and Lucy were seated in their hotel suite engaged in serious conversation. When Longarm entered the room, both women jumped up, and it wasn't hard to tell they wanted to know if he'd gotten any answers from Pete Black.

"Pete said that Lester's pistol was a .36-caliber Navy Colt."

"Then Dr. Maxwell lied!" Lucy exclaimed. "He must be one of the killers."

"No," Carole said, "it only means that he didn't know that Lester owned a Navy Colt and that the killer planted the .45 in Lester's hand after killing him."

"Carole is right," Longarm said. "Today, Dr. Maxwell is having Lester Gorton's body exhumed. He'll open up the cranium and extract the bullet that killed him. Then we'll learn what caliber of bullet was fired into Lester's head."

Lucy's brow furrowed. "Which will then tell us . . . what?"

"Lucy, these things are just like puzzles. You keep putting enough pieces down on the table and, sooner or later, you have something that makes sense. A *picture* emerges that makes everything clear."

"I see," Lucy said, looking as if she didn't see at all. "So what is our next move?"

"I'm going up to Virginia City," Longarm decided. "I can be up there by evening and try to see that lucky little girl that was the only one of her family to survive. I will also try to see Dan De Quille, who might be able to help shed some more light on what happened to the Wallaces."

"I'm coming too," Lucy said in a tone that left no room for discussion.

"And so will I," Carole announced.

"Well what about *your* newspaper job?" Longarm asked. "You do have a newspaper to put out, don't you?"

"Maybe I'll find a big story in Virginia City."

Longarm's response was quick and angry. "Oh, no, you don't! If you write this one up, I might as well go back to Denver and close the case."

"You wouldn't!"

"Watch me," Longarm vowed in a hard voice. "You can't do this, Carole. If and when I catch the murder or murderers, then you can have the story. That's the way it's got to be or it won't work."

93

Lucy nodded. "You can see how Custis's life would be jeopardized."

"All right," Carole agreed, "I won't go and I won't write anything on the case. But you have to keep me up to date on what you are finding. You have to promise that to me, Marshal. Otherwise. . . ."

"You have my word on it," Longarm said. "What is the fastest way up to Virginia City?"

"There's a stagecoach that leaves at noon, which you could catch, if you hurry. The next one leaves at four o'clock, and the last one at eight o'clock this evening. You could hire horses or your own driver and wagon, but that wouldn't get you there much faster and it will cost a fortune, which plenty of the newly rich miners can and are willing to pay."

"Where does the coach depart?"

"Two blocks below the river on Virginia Street. It's called the Hardwood Coach and Stables. Cost you five dollars each, if you can get a seat. The coach is always sold out so you might not."

"We'll get seats," Longarm vowed. He looked to his pocket watch. "But Lucy, I won't tolerate all that baggage. If you come with me, you come right now and you travel with just one satchel."

"Be reasonable!"

"I am being reasonable," Longarm said. "Are you coming or not?"

"I'm coming," Lucy snapped, grabbing up her biggest satchel and madly filling it with a change of clothes and her basic toiletries.

"Marshal," Carole said, "promise me that you'll come to my newspaper office the minute you return and fill me in on what you learn."

"I promise."

"All right, then," Carole said. "I have work of my own to do and they'll be fussing and wondering whatever happened to me this morning."

When Carole was gone, Lucy said, "Miss Shaw is a little strange, isn't she."

"How?"

"Well, she is nice and obviously bright, but she has so many sharp edges. She also walks and talks like a man."

"She's no man," Longarm said. "Far from it. But she has learned that, in order to make it in the newspaper business, a woman has to be fast and smart. I have little doubt that she faced a lot of opposition when she first went into what used to be a man's profession. Obviously, she has succeeded on her own terms."

"I hadn't thought of it that way," Lucy admitted. "And I'm sure that you're right. But she really isn't very attractive, is she."

"If you are talking like this out of jealousy, Carole already has a boyfriend. Now let's cut out the gossip and buy ourselves noon tickets to the Comstock Lode."

"I have heard so many exciting things about it," Lucy said as she stuffed the last of her belongings into the bulging satchel. "Custis, is Virginia City as wild and woolly as the stories would have everyone believe?"

"It's a real boom town. They call it the Big Bonanza, and I suppose that it is. Without a doubt, the Comstock Lode is the greatest silver and gold strike ever."

"Bigger than the Forty-Niner Rush in California?"

"Much, much bigger," Longarm said. "The Comstock Lode helped the Union finance the Civil War, and has attracted miners and capital from all over the world."

"My, you sure know a lot about things."

"No time for talk now, Lucy. I'll tell you more about the Comstock Lode once we're on that stagecoach and on our way up to Virginia City."

"Is it dangerous?"

"Yes," Longarm said. "If you're looking for trouble, you can sure find it aplenty on the Comstock."

"Aren't *we* looking for trouble?"

"We're looking for a lot more than trouble," Longarm told her as they left the room. "We're looking for the most evil man or group of lunatics that I've ever gone up against. That's why I expect you to let me do all the talking. Just keep your pretty eyes open and your ears to the ground."

"I'd rather keep my ears to a bed's mattress that we were making love on."

Longarm was surprised to hear such a brazen comment, but Lucy was all smiles as they swept out of the lobby and hurried on down Virginia Street toward the Hardwood Stables.

The noon stage was sold out.

"I'm sorry," the ticket agent, wearing a name badge saying "W. F. Boswell," said. "And I'm afraid that the four o'clock as well as the eight o'clock runs are sold out as well."

"Why the big rush to Virginia City?" Longarm asked.

"They're auctioning off several hundred thousand dollars of mining equipment. There's also some camel races and a boxing match this weekend. This is Friday and Virginia City is always crowded on the weekends. The town fathers and their Chamber of Commerce really keep the activities calendar filled."

"I'm glad for the town," Longarm said, "but we *really* need to be on that stagecoach."

"What can I tell you? The road up to Virginia City is a very hard pull and we have to keep the weight down to seven passengers, a modest amount of luggage, the driver, and a shotgun for protection. The best I can do is to sell you a ticket on the eight A.M. coach that leaves tomorrow morning."

"Won't do," Longarm flatly stated. "Mr. Boswell, would you please buy us two tickets?"

"Sir, are you asking me to repurchase them from my own customers?"

"That's right."

Boswell frowned and scratched his head. "I really would prefer not to do that. If you are that desperate to be on this coach, perhaps you could simply—"

"I don't want to draw any attention to ourselves," Longarm quietly explained. "And I don't want anyone who might like to sell their ticket to feel embarrassed. Do you understand?"

"Yes, this is awkward."

"It doesn't have to be," Longarm said, giving Boswell ten dollars. "Not if you handle the matter quietly. Now, is that enough to make it worth your trouble?"

"Oh, yes," Boswell said. "But how much are you willing to compensate for a pair of tickets on this coach?"

"As much as it takes," Longarm replied.

Boswell gazed around the livery yard where the ticketed passengers were gathered and waiting to board. "I think I see two miners who would gladly give up their tickets for . . . oh, ten dollars each plus the price of the tickets themselves, of course."

"Of course."

Longarm and Lucy watched with interest as Boswell went over to a pair of rough-looking miners. He took them aside and their conversation was very brief. A few moments later, Longarm met with them and their business was quickly concluded.

Ten minutes later, Longarm and Lucy were on their way up to the Comstock Lode. Their Conestoga coach had been stripped of all its extra weight and much of its traditional comforts because the trip was short and very steep. They rolled down South Virginia Street, and once out of town they passed small ranches and farms, until they finally arrived at the treacherous switchbacking road up to Virginia City.

"This will be slow going," Longarm said to no one in particular as the coach's speed was reduced to that of a man's walk.

"You were saying," Lucy began, "that the Comstock Lode is the largest gold and silver strike ever found."

"That's right," Longarm said. "It draws hardrock miners from around the world."

"What does that mean?"

Longarm studied a quiet miner seated opposite them and said, "Sir, perhaps you could explain hardrock mining to my wife."

"Me?" he asked with a definite Welsh accent. "Myself?"

"If you would be so kind."

The miner was in his early thirties, scrubbed and shaved. His hands were thick and powerful, and Longarm knew that they would be heavily calloused. He had a bad haircut that was either self-inflicted or given to him by a friend, and he wore a starched white collar that was too tight. His heavy work boots were worn down at the heels but polished. Longarm judged that the miner had probably gone to Reno to escape the temptations of wicked Virginia City for a few days, or even to do some fishing in the Truckee River. His impression was that the Irish and the Welsh especially loved to fish and missed flowing water.

"Well, ma'am, hardrock mining is different from placer mining, which is where you use a gold pan to wash color from the rivers. I've never done that, but I've heard about it often enough, and that was what they did in the Sierra Nevada gold fields."

"I see," Lucy said.

"But hardrock mining is *real* mining where we go deep down in the earth and dig out pockets of silver or gold—although you could do the same for copper or many other valuable metals."

"Do you climb down on long ladders?"

"Oh, no, ma'am! We are lowered in metal cages attached to cables that are powered by steam engines. We go down sometimes over a thousand feet where the air is as hot as . . . well, ma'am, it is very, very hot."

"It sounds awful!"

"It is," the Welshman agreed. "It is hot and dark and very dangerous. There are mine cave-ins all the time, and it is not uncommon for a man to sink his pick through a rock wall into a reservoir of boiling water."

The young miner sighed. "I have almost done that myself, and I've been on a level where it happened. It's a terrible thing to hear that boiling water burst through the rock and then to hear one of your friends screaming as he is scalded to death."

Lucy's hand flew to her mouth. "That happens?"

"Very often. Men and machinery also fall. Even a little rock kicked into the shaft to drop a thousand feet will kill a man quick as a bullet. Oh, it's dirty and dangerous work."

"Then why do you do it?"

"What else do I know? You see, I come from Wales, where our men are known as the finest hardrock miners in the world. There, I make one dollar a day, but here, thanks to the Miners Union, I make *five*! That's why I came all the way across the Atlantic Ocean and then across America."

"What if you. . . ." Lucy couldn't finish.

"If I am killed, as many are, then my friends will send all my savings home to my family. I have saved enough already that they could buy more farmland and never again be hungry."

"I see."

Lucy was moved by this story, which Longarm had heard so many times. Foreign miners by the thousands came to the American West to strike it rich, or at least set themselves and their families up for life. Most either died in accidents or of sickness, or else squandered their wages on women and drink, but this young man was obviously an exception.

"I will go home next year, God willing, ma'am. I've been here for five years and I've been very lucky. Last month, in the Ophir Mine, there was a fire that killed seven. I had just quit that crew for another. I think that God is watching over me, and I know that my mother and three sisters are praying for me every day."

"I'm sure that they are," Lucy said, reaching into her purse and digging out twenty dollars. "Here is a small gift."

The miner recoiled with embarrassment. He looked mortified and protested, "I do not accept charity!"

"Oh, it's *not* charity," Lucy said quickly. "And it's not for you. It's for your mother and three sisters."

"But you don't even know them!"

"Yes, I do," Lucy said. "Because you have told me of them and I know a little about you."

The miner looked to Longarm for help, but he smiled and said, "If you don't take the gift for your mother and sisters, my wife will just throw the twenty dollars out the window and someone will find and spend it all on whiskey."

The miner's hand came forward. "Could I tell them your name when I send this money?" he said in a voice thick with emotion.

"Lucy. Mrs. Lucy Long."

"God be with you, ma'am! This money is more than they can all earn working very hard for a month!"

Lucy abruptly turned her pretty face to the window, out toward the great Carson Valley and the rising vapors lifting off the mud pots and little steam geysers that never stopped bubbling. No one could see Lucy's averted face, but Longarm knew that it would be shining with tears.

Chapter 8

When their stagecoach finally crested a ridge, the driver pulled up and let the horses catch their wind. "You passengers might want to climb out and stretch your legs for about five minutes," he said. "Pretty nice view here."

Longarm really wasn't in the mood to enjoy a view, but he figured that he might as well climb out and look around. The ride up to this point had been nerve-racking because the road was so narrow that, when they met wagons coming down, passing was a tight squeeze with a margin of inches to spare.

"Oh, look at this!" Lucy exclaimed. "You can see part of Virginia City from here!"

"Yep," Longarm said, "we're only a few miles from it now. Off to the west you can see the Sierra Nevada Mountains and the grade we've been climbing all afternoon."

Lucy turned and stared back down into the Carson

Valley, which appeared to be at least two thousand feet below. It was beautiful, and off to the north she could see Reno. There was a warm breeze lifting off the valley, and it caused Lucy's skirts to riffle. Longarm figured that every man on this coach was thinking that the sight of Lucy was nearly as pretty as the natural scenery.

"I *like* this Nevada country," she said. "I even loved the desert and sagebrush part of it we crossed on the Union Pacific. But this is really beautiful."

"It has its own beauty," Longarm agreed. "But Nevada is a hard country with very hot summers and cold, windy winters. I'll stick with Colorado."

"I can't wait to see the Comstock Lode," Lucy said, turning to the southeast.

"I think you will find it everything you expect," Longarm told her. "Virginia City and its rival neighbor, Silver City, never sleep because the mines run twenty-four hours a day. That means that the saloons, dance halls, and gambling tables are crowded all the time."

"Is it lawless?"

"No. They've a marshal, and he has deputies to keep the peace. There has also been a very active vigilante committee for many years; and bad men are quickly captured and either run out off the Comstock or hanged. Most of the trouble is in the nature of theft, drunkenness, fighting, and other minor infractions of the law. There are shootouts, but knifings and robberies are far more common."

"I suppose that Virginia City, like almost all the mining towns, has its district for loose women."

"Yes, it does," Longarm said. "And there is a Chinatown just beyond a ridge separating Virginia City from Silver City. The Chinese have their ceremonial 'joss houses' where they gather and some people smoke opium pipes.''

"Opium?"

"Yes." Longarm frowned. "I've heard that opium is very popular in the Orient."

"Have you tried it?"

"Oh, hell, no. Rye whiskey is my favorite poison."

"All aboard," the driver called. "We'll be in Virginia City in one hour."

Longarm consulted his watch. "That means that we should arrive about seven o'clock. It will give us time to register in one of the nicer hotels, and then see if we can find that Wallace girl."

"What are you going to say to her?"

"I don't know," Longarm admitted. "Seeing as she was absent on the night that her family was lost in the fire, she probably doesn't know anything that will help us on this case. But I have to find out for certain. I'm pinning more of my hopes on Dan De Quille."

"I've heard of him. He was Mark Twain's friend and fellow worker on the *Territorial Enterprise*."

"That's right. And he's quite a character."

"Let's just hope that, when we point out to him the pattern of these murders, he realizes something that was not previously self-evident."

Longarm nodded in agreement, and they boarded the stage for the last few miles into Virginia City.

"My heavens!" Lucy exclaimed when they emerged from behind a sagebrush-covered hill. "Would you look at this!"

"You wouldn't expect anything so big and busy clear up in these barren hills, would you," Longarm said.

"No," Lucy agreed, her eyes wide with surprise because they were suddenly surrounded by immense hoisting works, wagons, and thousands of shacks, tents, and little mines marked by tailings that gave evidence to the depth of each shaft. "I never expected that the Comstock Lode was this big!"

The Welsh miner, who had earlier introduced himself as Alexander Dunn, said, "I work for the Savage Mine, one of the biggest and richest. But a lot of men come here, and when they can't get on a payroll, they just stake out a claim and start digging into the mountainside. Sometimes they strike a pocket of rich ore, but not very often. Most of it is buried hundreds of feet below the surface."

"It looks like a very hard life."

"Oh, it is, ma'am! The cemetery is large and growing every day. It's an especially bad place for women and children because it's so cold in the wintertime. The wind blows something awful up here and people die of pneumonia."

"Why are there no trees?"

Alexander Dunn was eager to display his knowledge of the Comstock. "They were all logged off many years ago. Most were used for square-set timbering, which is the way they support the mining shafts and tunnels. What wasn't strong enough for mine timbering was used in the wintertime for fuel."

"So where does the timbering and firewood come from now that it is all gone?"

"It is logged off the eastern slopes of the Sierras, some seventy or eighty miles away," Dunn explained. "They built V-shaped flumes, filled 'em with water, then the logs are sent down those wooden chutes all the way to the Carson River."

"That must be a sight!"

"It is, ma'am! Sometimes a drunken fool will climb onto one of those logs and ride it down the flume for a couple of miles! Usually, they are killed. Anyway, the logs float down the Carson river to sawmills that cut them into lumber and firewood. It's all hauled up Six Mile Canyon and it's frightfully expensive, ma'am."

"Then wood must be very expensive," Lucy said.

"*Everything* on the Comstock Lode is expensive," Dunn said, shaking his head. "Sure, our wages are high, but the prices are even higher. It's hard to save enough money to send home."

Longarm sat back and listened as the Welsh miner told Lucy about the rigors and dangers of living on the Comstock Lode. In Longarm's opinion, being a miner would be about the worst occupation imaginable. The idea of having to work a thousand feet under the ground in temperatures that approached 140 degrees was unimaginable. Besides that, Longarm had a tendency to suffer from claustrophobia, and working that far down in the bowels of the earth would be like crawling around in your own grave.

Their stage entered Virginia City on C Street, which was the main thoroughfare. As always, it was crowded and noisy, with its big, gaudy saloons like the Bucket of Blood and the Delta Queen. Lucy stared at all the activity and listened to the sounds of piano music pouring out of the halls. There were women on the sidewalks, and most of them had the look of dance hall girls or prostitutes.

"You had better stay close to your husband," Dunn warned Lucy. "There are churches, a school, and some very fine ladies living here, but they do not come down on C Street without being escorted, ma'am."

"I can see that," Lucy said as a miner and a prostitute

107

staggered up the street laughing and shouting obscenities while waving separate bottles of whiskey.

Their stagecoach made a sharp right turn off C Street and climbed a block up to B Street, then rolled into a livery. "Virginia City welcomes you, folks!"

Longarm helped Lucy out of the coach. The Welshman came up to them and shook Longarm's hand, before he turned to Lucy and bowed like a gentleman saying, "I will never forget your generosity. I promise that you will always be in my prayers and those of my family."

Lucy was visibly touched by his sincerity. Dunn was a handsome young man, even though his nose appeared to have been frequently broken and his hands were thick with scars. He had the look of a reformed brawler, of medium height, but with exceptional strength. He was quite a fine specimen of manhood, and he had obviously been raised to know his manners.

"Good-bye, ma'am," Dunn said, picking up a ragged valise. "And good luck to you, sir, on whatever endeavor has brought you and your wife to the Comstock Lode."

"Thanks," Longarm said, very much liking the cut of this young miner as he also wished him the best.

They collected their baggage and headed for a hotel that Longarm knew was nice as well as safe and respectable. He was concerned about having Lucy with him, and after noting her worried expression as they'd rolled into town, Longarm knew that she was apprehensive. Well, he thought, Lucy could either stay in her room while he was out and about, or else she would have to stay close by his side when he went to track down the Wallace girl and Dan De Quille.

As soon as they were registered at the hotel, Longarm

asked the short, efficient-looking desk clerk about the surviving Wallace girl.

"Oh, I'm afraid that little Annie Wallace isn't living on the Comstock anymore."

"She isn't?"

"No," the clerk said. "It is my understanding that Miss Wallace is living in Carson City with an aunt and an uncle. I'm not sure what their names are, but the girl was so distraught that everyone agreed that she would be better off leaving Virginia City and never returning."

"I see."

"Are you a friend or relative of the Wallace family?"

"A friend. I'd very much like to see Miss Wallace."

"I'm sure that she will be easy enough to find. Carson City isn't that big."

"Yes, well, it's dinnertime, and I also need to see Dan De Quille. Is he—"

"He could be anywhere," the desk clerk said. "He's always looking for a good story in the saloons or even on the sidewalks. I know where he can definitely be found tomorrow."

"Where?"

"He'll be covering the fights between our local toughs and a vicious bare-knuckles fighter named Hank Cutter. It costs twenty dollars to fight Cutter, but anyone still standing after three five-minute rounds will earn a hundred dollars."

"I've seen these professionals before," Longarm said. "Only once have I witnessed a challenger who lasted long enough to win the prize, and he used his winnings to pay his medical bills."

"Yes, Cutter will probably whip all comers. But there are some very hard-fisted men in this town don't know the meaning of fear or quit. There'll be at least four or five challengers tomorrow and a huge crowd. That's where you're sure to find Dan De Quille."

"When and where?"

"Tomorrow at noon down by the Virginia & Truckee Railroad depot. They've roped off a ring and set up bleachers. General admission is a dollar, ringside seats five dollars. I expect they'll sell out."

"Little doubt about that," Longarm said, knowing that these so-called "pugilistic exhibitions" were extremely popular even among respectable people, not to mention the not-so-respectable women who frequented the Comstock's saloons and whorehouses.

These fights were anticipated for weeks, and often talked about for years. Typically, some local favorite who worked as a miner, logger, or cowboy would get about half drunk and then, at the urging of his friends, foolishly agree to step into the ring with someone far more skilled in the hope of displaying his strength and courage. The local favorite would be hoping to win fame and a little fortune, not to mention the hearts of admiring women. However, these fights tended to average less than one complete round because a real professional like Hank Cutter would be vastly superior in his ability and conditioning. With just a few thundering and well-placed blows, Cutter would quickly reduce the local hero to a shambling, bloodied punching bag.

The outcomes were hardly ever in doubt. If the challenger were smart or had any remaining wits after being knocked half senseless, he would abandon his foolish pride and dive for safety between the ropes, causing a great deal of laughter among the spectators. But those challengers too dazed or stupid to give up would be beaten to the ground, and often had to be carried out on a stretcher.

Longarm escorted Lucy to dinner in the hotel's fine dining room, then took her back up to their room with the full intention of excusing himself and going out on the town in search of Dan De Quille. Lucy, however, had an entirely different plan.

"I want you to stay here with me tonight," she said, unbuttoning his shirt and then kissing his chest. "I want you to make love to me over and over."

"Oh, yeah?"

She peeled off his shirt. "That's right."

Longarm had to admit that he wasn't really in the mood to join the Comstock crowds prowling saloon after saloon in search of Dan De Quille. Their hotel room was plush and the bed looked very inviting. They had enjoyed wine with their dinner and an apricot brandy with their dessert. And now, as Lucy unbuttoned his pants and found his manhood, Longarm discovered it was very easy to cave in to her wishes.

He began to kiss her face and her hair. Soon, they were both tearing off their clothes and falling into bed. Lucy could be a lady among ladies, but in bed she was a tigress. Longarm heard her gasp and moan with pleasure as his tongue laved her nipples until they were as hard and wrinkled as raisins. Lucy reached for his throbbing manhood and giggled. "Oh, Custis, let's make this a night to remember!"

"Fine with me," he said as his finger slipped into her moist honeypot and Lucy began to writhe at his expert touch. He stroked and licked her until she was yanking so hard on his cock that he knew it was time to get down to the real business of making love.

"Open wide," he grunted, burying his stiff rod into her womanhood.

"Oh, honey!" she cried, wrapping her legs around

his hips and grabbing his buttocks with both hands as he began to thrust. "Harder!"

Longarm gave Lucy everything he had. She begged for more, so he grabbed a satin-encased pillow and slipped it under her lovely hips, and then thrust even deeper and harder.

"Oh, honey!" she cried, as she began to lose control of herself and thrash under his relentless pounding. "Oh, yes!"

Longarm felt Lucy's body stiffen, and that was when his own seed began to spew like hot lava while they clutched and slammed at each other until they finally extinguished their inner fires.

Longarm made love to Lucy twice more before midnight. Each time took a little longer, and that seemed to please Lucy.

Just before falling into an exhausted sleep, Longarm said, "I'm going to see Dan De Quille at the pugilistic exhibitions tomorrow at noon."

"Everyone is talking about them," Lucy whispered, pressing tight against him. "I want to come."

"I don't think you'd like it."

"Why? Do you still think I'm too delicate? Too much the sheltered young Denver lady?"

"These 'exhibitions' get pretty bloody. Men are hurt and it is anything but a pretty sight."

"I want to see things that I haven't seen before," Lucy whispered in the darkness. "I *have* been sheltered, to a certain extent. And while I do not want to see men hurt men, I'd like to go to one of these things just once and try to figure out their fascination."

"Lucy, I just don't—"

"I'm going, darling. With or without you. There are

going to be other respectable women in attendance, aren't there?''

"Yes."

"Then take me and protect me from the wolves. Besides, I've read many articles by the great Dan De Quille and I'd like to finally meet him. And there is always the slight chance that I might pick up something he says about the Wallace murders that you'll miss.''

"Not very likely. But okay, I'll take you.''

"Thank you, Custis. And don't worry about me and the fights. I've seen men fight before. I wasn't raised in a convent, you know.''

"Maybe you have seen a fistfight or two,'' Longarm told her. "As pretty as you are, I'd even expect that you *caused* a few fistfights.''

"No.'' She giggled. "At least none that I knew about.''

"Well,'' Longarm said, "what you will see down at the Virginia & Truckee Railroad station is unlike anything you've seen before. These so-called exhibitions will be between men, not boys, and they will be fast and furious. The local challengers almost never win, but sometimes they do get in a lucky punch and come out of the fray victorious.''

"Have you ever gotten into the ring with one of these professionals?''

"No,'' Longarm said, "but once I did have a friend who made his living traveling about and doing these things. He was a big Irishman named Jake McCall, and he could hit like the kick of a mule with either hand. He could also take a hard punch. That's why he lasted so long in the profession before he was killed.''

"What happened?''

"I wasn't there,'' Longarm said, "but I was told by

reliable witnesses that, after Jake whipped the local favorite and collected his winnings, he was shot to death and robbed.''

"What a shame!''

"Yeah,'' Longarm agreed. "It was funny. Out of the ring, Jake was a gentle Irish giant. But inside, he turned into something that I never knew or understood. He was two different men, Lucy, and the few times that I saw him fight I hardly recognized him. Something came into his eyes that I can only describe as dementia. Or . . . or some kind of insane fury. He just seemed to go berserk in the ring.''

"Are there no rules?

"There are supposed to be,'' Longarm said. "You're not supposed to be able to gouge an eye, bite, or kick an opponent, but that happens all the time. There usually isn't a referee in attendance, only a doctor.''

"It sounds extremely violent.''

"That's what I'm trying to tell you, Lucy. So if you insist on going, don't faint or throw up on me.''

"I won't.''

"Promise me that you will close your eyes if you start to feel sick. Or let me know and we'll leave immediately. I can always go back and find Dan De Quille.

"All right.'' Lucy yawned. "I promise.''

Longarm reached down and kissed her large, soft breasts, thinking it might be nice to make love to this lovely but complex lady one more time. But then he heard Lucy's soft breathing, and knew that she had already fallen asleep.

Chapter 9

It was a perfect day for a fight, and Longarm went down
to the train depot early in order to purchase ringside
tickets while Lucy was still asleep. He was surprised that
a sizeable crowd was already gathered and a good many
of the cheap seats already occupied.

Longarm spotted the ticket booth and went over to
buy a pair of seats. The man selling the tickets beamed
and said, "Ten dollars, please. When you see Hammerin' Hank Cutter, you'll be seeing the finest pugilist
in America."

"How are ticket sales going?"

"Hey," the fat little man chewing on the stub of a
large black cigar said, "I couldn't ask for any more.
Hammerin' Hank and I will probably clear three to five
hundred dollars on the ticket sales alone. I just hope that
we get plenty of game challengers."

"What if you don't?"

The man shrugged, then jacked his thumb toward a

poster. ''If we don't, that poster says that Hank Cutter will get into the ring and shadow box for three five-minute rounds.''

''And that's it?''

''That's it,'' the promoter said. ''And while we have had a few times where not one single man had the guts to fight, it's rare. Hammerin' Hank isn't especially big. I mean, he's six foot and weighs an even two hundred thirty, but he's no giant and he doesn't scare challengers away because of his appearance. There are always plenty of bigger men in the crowd. Men like you. Say, why don't *you* fight Hammerin' Hank?''

''No, thanks,'' Longarm said, taking his tickets. ''The prize isn't worth my teeth, or some broken ribs.''

''You look to be in good shape. Maybe a little too light for your height, but strong.''

''I prefer to watch other men learn that an amateur *never* beats a professional.''

The promoter chuckled. ''Well, I can see that you're not going to fight, so just enjoy the show while I take care of these other folks who need tickets.''

Longarm turned and spotted Dan De Quille standing off by himself. The *Territorial Enterprise* reporter was tall and slender, with uncombed black hair and penetrating eyes that had probably seen too much of the dark side of life. He was known for his wit and his prose, but also for his hard drinking. Longarm had met him a few times, and now he went up and introduced himself.

''I remember you,'' Dan said. ''Marshal—''

''I'd appreciate it if you just called me Custis,'' Longarm said quickly. ''I'm here working on a murder case and it would hurt my chances of solving it if everyone knew that I was a lawman.''

''Of course,'' De Quille agreed, slipping his pad and

pencil into his black frock coat. "Would you mind telling me what this case is all about?"

"Have you a few moments to spare so that we can talk in private?"

"Certainly! I was just waiting to interview Hammerin' Hank Cutter, but he probably won't arrive for a while. He's supposed to be pure meanness and so I'm not very anxious to speak to him, but my readers expect the interview, so I have no choice."

Longarm took De Quille aside and quickly explained why he had come to the Comstock Lode and what kind of a man he was trying to apprehend. As he listened, De Quille's eyes grew ever wider with amazement.

"And you actually believe that Mr. Wallace and his family died at the hands of this Rebel Executioner?"

"I do," Longarm said. "And so does Miss Carole Shaw who writes for the Reno paper. Actually, she is the one that has tied all these seemingly unrelated deaths and suicides together."

"My goodness, do you think that little Annie Wallace might be in mortal danger?"

"No," Longarm answered, "but I can't be entirely sure because we are dealing with someone who is probably insane. That's why, after I leave Virginia City and return to Reno, I'll be visiting her in Carson City."

"If you need help, any help at all . . ."

"I do," Longarm said. "Miss Shaw showed me the fine article you wrote on the Wallace family. It was a beautiful eulogy and a tribute to that prominent Virginia City family."

De Quille accepted the praise with obvious satisfaction, but there was a hint of deep sadness when he said, "They were an exceptional family, and I gave the article the very best that I had to give."

"It showed," Longarm said. "I hope that now that I've made you aware that we are probably dealing with a murderer or group of murderers, you will turn the entire sad affair over a few extra times in your mind and maybe come up with something . . . some clue that will help me identify the killer or killers."

"I see." De Quille frowned. "Well, to be honest, I can't think of anything that might lead toward a good suspect. Fires are quite common, and most of the structures on the Comstock Lode are, unfortunately, made of wood. In the case of the Wallace family, the prevailing theory is that a cat knocked over a kerosene lamp."

"A cat?"

"That's correct," De Quille said. "The Wallace family loved cats. They collected strays. In the summertime they roamed about outside, but on especially cold days, the cats would be allowed inside. Annie told me that on at least two occasions, cats knocked over kerosene lamps and caused some minor fire damage."

"Then why didn't they . . . well, take precautions?"

"They *loved* cats," De Quille answered. "Annie said that her father gave orders that no kerosene lamps were to be used unless someone was in the room when a cat was present. But this fire started just before daybreak, and I think it quite probable that a cat had slipped inside the Wallace home and that a flickering lamp was overturned by the feline."

Longarm expelled a deep breath. "That makes sense. However, I'm sure that this tragedy was *not* caused by a cat. Mr. Wallace was a Union War hero, and the similarities between his death and those of other victims I've been reading about are just too closely related. Dan, please go over your notes or whatever you have in order to help me on this case."

"I most certainly will just as soon as I have written this piece on Hammerin' Hank Cutter. I'm praying that he does *not* live up to his reputation."

"It's bad, huh?"

"Cutter has maimed and even *killed* men in the ring. I hope that this audience has a very strong stomach and that no one challenges Cutter. My article today strongly condemns this so-called 'exhibition' and implores everyone to boycott it."

"Obviously that is not going to happen," Longarm said, gazing around at the excited and growing audience.

"No," De Quille said, "but I hadn't expected them to. However, I did write up a little chronology on Hank Cutter listing the men he has either killed or permanently crippled. I would be gratified if no one here today would enter that ring and these blood-letting, blood-sucking parasites would simply leave the Comstock after putting on their little circus act."

"Well," Longarm said, "I guess I'll be going back up to the hotel. We've got ringside tickets and. . . ."

"Who is *we*?"

"I'm traveling with Mrs. Long."

"Congratulations!"

Longarm did not see any point in telling the reporter that Lucy wasn't really his wife, so he just nodded and started to leave, but De Quille's voice suddenly caused him to change his mind.

"Ah!" the reported exclaimed. "If it isn't the great Hammerin' Hank Cutter! I am Dan De Quille of the *Territorial Enterprise,* and I'd like to interview you prior to this afternoon's exhibition."

Cutter was far bigger and more threatening than described by his promoter. The man stood nearly as tall as Longarm, and his head was shaved. Cutter was brutish, with deep-set and pitiless eyes, a fist-flattened nose, and a square, scarred face that gave testimony to the fact that he had been fighting for many, many years. His physique was a mystery at the moment, because he was wearing a long black robe made of satin with his name sewn in big yellow letters across the chest. Even so, Longarm could tell that he was very thick and solid. Very powerful.

"You the one that wrote about me in today's paper?" Cutter demanded of the renowned Comstock reporter.

"Why yes, but . . ."

Hank Cutter reached out, grabbed De Quille with his left fist, and dragged him up close so that they were almost touching noses. "You skinny sonofabitch!" Cutter hissed. "I ought to break your damned neck!"

Longarm stepped forward saying, "I think that would be a very bad idea, Cutter."

"Who the hell are you?" the pugilist demanded, tossing the reporter aside as if he were a ruined rag doll.

"I'm Dan De Quille's friend."

Cutter's eyes narrowed. "You gonna do something more than talk, mister?"

Longarm knew that the pugilist expected him to lose his nerve and began to wheedle out of this confrontation. Instead, Longarm drew his six-gun in a swift motion and jabbed its barrel into Cutter's bull neck. He jabbed so hard that Cutter, moving forward, was brought up short and choking.

"You step away and apologize to Mr. De Quille or you'll be damned sorry."

"You wouldn't shoot me."

"Try me, you ugly bastard."

Cutter and Longarm locked eyes, and it was Cutter

who finally looked away muttering out of the side of his mouth, "Sorry, you hack."

Longarm doubted that he would get any more of an apology from this man, so he holstered his gun.

Cutter turned back to him and said, "You're real tough when you're up against an unarmed man. How about stepping into the ring with me this afternoon and we find out how tough you really are?"

"I don't think so."

"That's because, without your gun, you're just a big chicken-shit sonofabitch," Cutter hissed.

Longarm knew that the professional fighter was baiting him, but he wasn't taking that bait. Instead, he turned and started walking away, hearing Hank Cutter scorning him. It really rankled him, but Longarm knew that it was better to walk away from this fight. The President of the United States of America was counting on him to solve the case of the Rebel Executioner. Longarm figured losing a little bit of face was small change compared to doing the job that he had been sent to do by Billy Vail and the President.

Longarm found Lucy waking up in their hotel room. He told her about his meeting with Dan De Quille, and ended by saying, "Dan says the prevailing theory about that Wallace mansion fire was that it was caused by a cat knocking over a kerosene lamp."

"A cat!"

"That was the way I reacted," Longarm said, filling in the story with the same details he'd received from Dan de Quille. "And to be honest, it's a very logical explanation for the cause of that fire."

"But we both know that it was set deliberately!"

"No," Longarm corrected, "we both *suspect* that it was set deliberately, but we don't have proof to back up our suspicions. That's the rub. And without proof, we really can't say or do a thing, Lucy.''

"Do you think that Mr. De Quille will be able to help us?"

"No," Longarm said, "I do not. But he promised to go over his notes and jog his memory. He was quite sympathetic about the tragedy, and I think I convinced him that there very well could a sinister plot behind these deaths. He was also quite concerned about Annie Wallace."

"Who is in Carson City."

"Yes. I think, after we return to Reno, I need to go down and see that little girl."

"Do you believe her life is actually in danger?"

"Not really, but what if I am wrong?"

Lucy actually shuddered at the thought. "Maybe we should leave on the next coach to Reno."

"No," Longarm decided, "let's see the fight and then give Mr. De Quille at least a few hours to ruminate on what I've told him of our suspicions."

"All right."

"By the way," Longarm said, "I had the displeasure of meeting Hammerin' Hank Cutter. He has the eyes of a reptile, and I've rarely seen a face so scarred or brutal-looking. I'm afraid that we did not have a friendly discussion."

"Maybe he'll get whipped today," Lucy said hopefully.

"I very much doubt that, but miracles sometimes happen."

It was just a few minutes before noon when Longarm and Lucy arrived at ringside. Longarm was relieved to see that there were quite a few other women besides

Lucy in attendance. Their seats were about three rows back, and they had to show their tickets in order to take their places. All the while, Lucy was clinging to Longarm as if he were a life buoy and she were adrift at sea.

"If you've changed your mind," Longarm said, "I will escort you back to our hotel room."

"No," Lucy said, "because I doubt I'll ever see anything like this again."

"Or want to," Longarm said cryptically.

"Oh, my heavens, is that him?" Lucy exclaimed, her hand flying up to cover her open mouth.

Longarm followed her eyes, and then he nodded. "Yep. That's Hammerin' Hank Cutter."

"He's . . . he's terrible!"

"This is not a little boy's birthday party, Lucy."

"I hope no one fights him. I . . . I don't even want to see what he can do with his fists."

Hammerin' Hank Cutter ducked under the single strand of rope that defined the ring. He turned full circle, sneering as the crowd of at least five hundred booed him lustily. Then Cutter removed his robe and flexed his muscles. The boisterous crowd fell silent and gaped at the man's body, which appeared to have been chiseled out of solid marble.

"Look at that!" Lucy whispered. "I never knew that a man could be so . . . so strong. There's not an ounce of fat on his entire body. He's amazing."

"He's a pure, unadulterated ass," Longarm snapped.

"Ladies and gentleman," the promoter shouted as he bounced into the ring with a megaphone. "This is the time that you have all been waiting for—the hour of doom . . . or destiny! Doom for those who would fight for glory but lose . . . destiny for anyone good enough to beat Hammerin' Hank Cutter and win the prize as well

123

as becoming a legend in his own time! Yes, a legend!''

The promoter let the word ''legend'' sink in slowly, and then he cried, ''So who believes it is *their* destiny to achieve everlasting fame, fortune, and glory today?''

Several men jumped to their feet, shouting and raising their fists. Longarm dismissed them at a single glance. They were all feeding on excitement and whiskey courage. They might be strong and tough, but not a one of them belonged in a ring with the likes of Hank Cutter.

''You!'' the promoter shouted, pointing to one of the men. ''What is your name?''

''Marco Petri! And I come to win!''

''Well, come on, come on! Let's see what you can do!''

Petri was a big, strapping Italian, maybe six feet tall and obviously very strong. He was good-looking, but there was also a toughness about him that was immediately apparent when he charged up the aisle and climbed into the ring. He ripped off his shirt, and his torso was impressive, with layers of rippling muscle. Waving to his friends in the crowd, who cheered him as they might a hero, he posed with his fists up and his chin tucked down tight against his chest.

''Are you ready to fight?'' the promoter shouted.

Petri stopped posing and his smile died as he stared across the ring at Hank Cutter. ''Yeah, I'm ready!''

What happened next was hard to believe. One minute Petri was moving forward with his fists up; the very next he was being knocked senseless and blood was pouring from his nose, his mouth, and both ears. Rarely had even Longarm seen such savage fury as was exhibited by Hammerin' Hank Cutter. The man's powerful arms moved like locomotive pistons as they drilled Petri's face and body until both were a mass of crimson. Petri's friends now stood ashen-faced as their young gladiator crumpled like a wet newspaper and collapsed to his knees.

Hank Cutter grinned viciously and measured his helpless opponent.

"No!" Longarm shouted. "He's finished!"

But *Cutter* wasn't finished. He hit Petri so hard with a right uppercut that the young man was lifted three inches off the ground, and everyone in the audience heard the crack of breaking bone as Petri was knocked over backward.

Cutter raised his arms and began to dance around in a circle. He hardly seemed to have broken a sweat. And then he did something that really infuriated Longarm. He placed his foot on the unconscious Petri's neck and pumped it hard so that Petri's body had a violent spasm and he spat fresh blood.

"I'm going to get sick!" Lucy cried, leaping to her feet.

"You bloody bastard, fight me!" a voice arose from somewhere in the stunned audience.

Longarm turned to see the young Welshman, Alexander Dunn, marching toward the ring.

"Oh, no!" Lucy cried, trying to reach Dunn before he entered the ring, but unable to do so because she was restrained by Longarm.

Dunn ignored the promoter and, without introduction and with Petri still lying in the center of the ring coughing up blood, he attacked Hank Cutter with such fury that the professional was actually obliged to back up and defend himself. Cutter suffered a deep laceration over his right eye, and took several thundering punches to the face and belly, before he charged forward and began to beat back Dunn's frenzied challenge. And then, with the crowd going crazy, both men stood toe to toe for almost a full minute trading punches, until Alexander Dunn took a thundering blow to the point of his jaw and was knocked out cold.

"Thank God he was knocked out," Longarm shouted to Lucy over the roar of the crowd, "or else Cutter would have broken his face and body up the same way he did with young Petri."

And that might have been the end of the exhibit except that Hammerin' Hank Cutter jumped up in the air and landed on Dunn's chest. Fortunately, he didn't land squarely, and so his ankles turned and he tumbled to his knees. By then, Longarm was already out of his seat, bowling over rows of spectators and diving under the ring rope.

"Hey!" he shouted, wanting nothing more than to distract Hank Cutter before he broke every rib in Dunn's chest.

Hank Cutter swung around, his eyes gleaming with blood lust. When he recognized Longarm he actually giggled, and then he raised his massive arms and roared.

Longarm didn't have time to remove his shirt or even his gun and cartridge belt. Hank attacked like a charging buffalo, and it was all that Longarm could do to duck under his punches and bounce on the toes of his feet, raising his fists while desperately trying to remember all the lessons that he'd been taught by Jake McCall, the big Irish fighter who had once been every bit as good as Hank Cutter.

Custis, the Irishman seemed to say across the years, *if you're damn sure he's stronger and hits harder, then box him, confuse him, but don't stand toe to toe and slug it out with him! And if he ever nails you with a haymaker, try to hit him coming in where it will do the most damage, or he will beat your fuckin' brains out.*

Those were the wise words of advice given to Longarm by the Irishman, and now he attempted to apply them. In addition to offense, Longarm had also learned something of defense, and those lessons came in handy as he warded off Cutter's furious onslaught, catching most of the pugilist's punches on his elbows, forearms, and even his broad shoulders.

Cutter was grunting with each blow delivered and taken, and he was taking plenty. Longarm was hitting him from every angle and with every punch he had ever learned. Right crosses, left jabs to the eyes and mouth, then whistling uppercuts that hurt badly. But Hank was also landing. In fact, Longarm had never been hit this hard, and his forearms were becoming so numb that he knew he wouldn't be able to defend himself much longer.

Longarm drove an uppercut from down near his knees, and that caught Hank Cutter exactly at the point of his jaw. The professional's legs finally buckled and the crowd went crazy. Longarm swarmed all over Cutter. He thought that he could hear Lucy screaming, but he was not sure because his ears were ringing and one of his eyes was already swollen half shut.

Cutter drove a knee up between Longarm's legs that should have ended the fight, but Longarm just barely managed to twist sideways and protect his most vulnerable parts. Somehow, he grabbed Cutter's knee and then kicked the man's leg out from under him. Taking a lesson from the professional, he landed on Cutter's chest with his own drawn knees, not giving a damn if he broke every one of the sonofabitch's ribs.

Cutter's breath exploded from his lungs, and before he could regain his wind, Longarm grabbed one of his ears and pinned the man's face to the earth. Then he punched the pugilist again and again.

"I give up!" Hank screamed. "No more!"

Longarm climbed to his feet and staggered out of the ring into Lucy's arms. After that, he didn't remember anything because he passed out cold.

Longarm didn't awaken until the following morning, when a bespectacled doctor roused him with smelling salts. "I was the attending physician at yesterday's fights," the doctor said. "I've never been so happy to see a man beaten in my life as I was when you whipped Hammerin' Hank Cutter."

"I feel like he whipped me."

"You have some pretty severe bruises and more than a couple of lacerations. But compared to Hank Cutter, you are in remarkably good condition."

"What about Alexander Dunn?"

"Broken jaw, I'm afraid. He's going to be out of work for quite some time."

"Don't worry about him," Lucy said, coming into view. "I've already sent word to his friends that I will contribute to his welfare, matching any donations that they can raise."

"What about *my* welfare?" Longarm asked through puffy lips.

"You'll be well taken care of," Lucy said sweetly.

The doctor said, "The man who suffered the most physical damage was that young Petri. I'm afraid that he was beaten quite severely."

"We'll be glad to help him out as well," Lucy vowed. "Won't we, Custis?"

"Sure," Longarm said. "I'll donate my ring prize to him."

"When I was attending Hank Cutter," the doctor said, "he told me that he had never been beaten like that before. What you did to him was almost as vicious as what he's been doing to other men. Cutter told me to tell you that he didn't hold any grudges for ending his fighting career."

"That's nice to know," Longarm said. "Although I still believe that the man ought to be hanged."

"He might be changed," the physician said hopefully. "Once a man is beaten that badly, it's not likely that he'll come back to the ring again. You nearly killed Hammerin' Hank. He wants to know who taught you how to fight like a professional."

"Tell him it was a big Irishman by the name of Jake McCall. Hank will recognize the name, and then he'll understand why he finally got to taste some of his own bitter medicine."

"Custis," Lucy pleaded, "promise me that you'll never get into a prizefighting ring again."

"I promise, and that's the easiest promise I'll ever make," he replied. "Lucy, we need to get back to Reno."

"That's impossible," the doctor informed them. "You'll have trouble just sitting up for the next two days and chewing soft foods."

Longarm knew better than to argue with this physician. So he nodded his head and closed his one good eye before he went back to sleep.

Chapter 10

"Mr. Long!" Dan De Quille exclaimed as he stepped into the hotel room where Longarm was convalescing. "I apologize for dropping in like this without an appointment, but . . ."

"Never mind that," Longarm said. "Lucy, this is the famous Dan De Quille."

"At your service," the Comstock journalist said, bowing slightly.

"I'm interested in names," Lucy said. "Is Dan De Quille your *real* name?"

"It's just my pen name. My real name is William Wright. Mark Twain is also a pen name used by my friend and former associate Samuel Clemens."

"I see," Lucy said. "Well, I think you *both* were very wise to use such interesting pen names. Not that there is anything wrong with William or Samuel. Its just that the names you've chosen are *far* more interesting."

"Dear," Longarm said, trying to hide his exasperation over Lucy's nonsensical prattle, "I'm sure that Mr. De Quille has not come to talk about names."

"No," Dan said. "As a matter of fact . . . may I sit down?"

"Of course! Lucy, please drag that chair over to my bedside for Dan."

"No, no! I'll do it," De Quille said.

When he was seated beside the bed, he bent forward and made a steeple of his long fingers before using them to rest his pointed chin. "Mr. Long, first I want to tell you that I have never been so surprised . . . and gratified as when you whipped Hank Cutter to within an inch of his miserable life. Like nearly everyone else in attendance, I almost yelled myself hoarse cheering for you. If ever overdue justice was administered, it was yesterday in that boxing ring."

"Thank you," Longarm said, "but . . ."

"I hope that you have a very complete and speedy recovery. Also, I wanted you to know that I did not use your true identity in the article that will come out in today's edition of the *Territorial Enterprise* recalling your famous fight."

"That is appreciated."

"However, you are now quite the most interesting and mysterious man on the entire Comstock Lode! Everyone is nearly rabid to know your name and true identity. Are you aware that, at this very moment, there are legions of adoring fans waiting outside this hotel to catch a glimpse of you?"

"No."

"It's true. And the fact that I did not reveal your name or identity heightens the mystery and curiosity of my readers."

Longarm shook his head. "The very last thing I need

is fanfare or publicity, Dan.'' He turned to Lucy. ''We're going to have to sneak out of this hotel and find a way back down to Reno.''

''What a pity!'' De Quille exclaimed.

''Not to me it isn't,'' Longarm said. ''And compared to what is at stake regarding the murders of former Union heroes and soldiers, what happened in that ring yesterday means nothing.''

''You are absolutely correct, sir! Now, then, let's get down to what is really important. Before you made pugilistic history yesterday, you asked me to give the matter of the Wallace tragedy the full power of my intellect. I have done so and come up with what I believe might be very important information.''

Longarm felt his pulse quicken. He glanced over at Lucy and saw that she was holding her breath. Longarm nodded and said, ''Go on.''

''I remembered that the Wallace family had a *guest* in their mansion at the time of the fire. That in itself was not remarkable because the family often had company, but this guest vanished!''

''What do you mean?'' Lucy asked.

''His body was never found in the ashes!'' De Quille exclaimed. ''The others all were accounted for and identified, but not the remains of the guest.''

''Who was this mystery visitor?'' Longarm asked, scarcely daring to believe that he could get so lucky.

''I have no idea,'' De Quille admitted. ''I never met him, never even saw him, but only knew of his existence because Annie told me there was a guest in her house when it caught on fire. Some 'friend' of her father.''

''I don't suppose she gave you his name.''

''His name was Allen. Annie called him Mr. Allen. Now, that could have been his first name, or his last.

133

Also, he might simply have departed on the day before the inferno that razed the Wallace mansion.''

Longarm shook his head. "If he had, the likelihood is that he would have heard about the tragedy and returned to offer support or help.''

"Not necessarily so,'' De Quille countered. "He might have, for example, simply boarded a train or a stagecoach, or even his own horse, and left hours before the fire. It seems quite possible to me that he could have gone merrily on his way and not be aware of the terrible tragedy even now.''

"Mr. De Quille is right,'' Lucy said, looking at Longarm. "Isn't he right?''

"Yes,'' Longarm reluctantly agreed, "he is. But I think that this 'Mr. Allen' should become our main suspect.''

"How,'' De Quille asked, "can you possibly find him?''

"First,'' Longarm said, "I need to know more about him. To do that, I have to talk to Annie Wallace.''

"Are you still certain that her life is not in danger?'' De Quille asked.

"No,'' Longarm said, "I am not. In fact, if Annie can identify our mysterious Mr. Allen, then I think it quite likely that her life is very much in danger.''

Longarm swung his feet out of the bed, grunting in pain. "I need to question and protect that girl as soon as possible.''

"I'm going with you,'' Lucy declared.

"I just *wish* that I could go with you,'' De Quille lamented. "But I simply can't. However, I can arrange for a driver and a carriage to be brought around to the back of this hotel so that you can get away without attracting any attention.''

"That would be very much appreciated," Longarm said.

"The doctor said that you should stay in bed for at least a few days," Lucy said. "Custis, are you sure you feel well enough to travel?"

"Have I any choice if a fourteen-year-old girl's life is in jeopardy?"

"No," Lucy said. "We'd better hurry."

Longarm reached out and shook De Quille's hand. "Thank you for remembering what could make the difference between more people living or dying."

"My God," De Quille whispered. "I just hope that I didn't remember too late to save Annie!"

"Me too," Longarm agreed. "Do you recall the name of the aunt and uncle she was taken in by?"

"Yes. Now that it has become so important, I do. They were Dutch people, and I recall that they were very nice and own a dairy just outside town."

"Their names."

"Zalstra. Mr. and Mrs. Zalstra."

"I'll find them without any trouble at all," Longarm said.

"How many Zalstras can there be in a place the size of Carson City?"

"Very few, I'd imagine."

Dan De Quille left promising to have a carriage waiting for them behind the hotel in less than an hour. Longarm, his ribs so tender that each step was a torment, managed to get dressed with Lucy's help. It didn't take them much more than thirty or forty minutes to pack up their bags and sneak down the rear fire escape. Fortunately, the carriage was ready and waiting.

They paid off the driver and used the back streets until they topped the Divide, and then joined the heavy flow of traffic moving up and down Gold Hill Canyon on the way through Silver City and on down to Carson City. It was perhaps twenty-five miles between the Comstock and Nevada's capital, but it seemed like a hundred to Longarm. When they reached the town, they drove past the silver-domed capitol building and the impressive senate and assembly chamber buildings.

"Where are we going to get directions to the Zalstra dairy?" Lucy asked.

In reply, Longarm started questioning everyone within shouting distance, and because Carson City was quite small and with a permanent resident population, as opposed to the boom towns, they had no trouble getting directions. The dairy was just a mile north of the capital, nestled tight up against the base of the Sierras.

Longarm pushed the carriage horses hard, and they were really puffing by the time that they arrived at the Zalstra dairy.

"Dear God," Lucy breathed, "please don't let us be too late to save the Wallace girl."

And then, just as if her prayer was answered, they saw Annie Wallace emerge from the dairy barn carrying a pail of milk with three or four mewing cats in tow.

"Thank you, Lord!" Lucy breathed. "Custis, that *has* to be her, doesn't it?"

"I'm sure that it is."

When the girl saw them, she smiled and waved with her free hand. Longarm drove their carriage up to a hitching rail and dismounted stiffly, wincing with pain. He tied the team, and then Lucy came to join him as a large, fair-haired woman wearing an apron emerged from the house.

"If you want to buy fresh cream or milk, you should go to the barn where my husband will help you."

136

"We're not here to buy anything," Longarm said, knowing that his bruised face might cause this woman alarm. "We're here to talk to Miss Annie Wallace."

The woman hurried over to Annie and slipped her arm protectively around her. "She has nothing to say to anyone. She's been through enough, so you just go away!"

Before Longarm or Lucy could react, the woman was ushering Annie into the house and slamming the door in their wake.

"Something must have happened to upset them," Longarm said.

"Maybe it's your face."

"No, it's more than that." Longarm glanced toward the barn, and caught a glimpse of a large man who had been watching them but had now disappeared. "Lucy, let's talk to Mr. Zalstra and explain why we've come and why we believe that Annie's life is in danger."

Mr. Zalstra was milking a large fawn-colored cow when they entered the barn, which smelled of fresh cow shit and alfalfa. There were at least twenty more cows waiting to be milked, but Longarm went right up to the man and said, "Mr. Zalstra, I'm a United States deputy marshal and I believe that Annie Wallace is in danger."

The Dutchman had immense hands and with each tug on a teat, a long squirt of frothy milk streamed into a pail. He twisted his head around to study Longarm.

"You don't look like an officer of the law to me. You look like a rounder."

"I know," Longarm said, reaching into his coat pocket for his badge and dragging it out, "but I am a law officer and have identification to prove it."

Zalstra came off his stool and studied the badge. "Could be anyone's," he said finally. "I've even seen them for sale in pawnshops."

"All right then," Longarm replied, "have you ever seen a letter from the President of the United States on his *official stationery*?"

Zalstra shook his head. He was in his fifties, tall and cadaverous, with sunken eyes and prominent cheekbones. His complexion was very pale, and so were his blue eyes as he studied the letter that gave Longarm the power to do just about anything he needed to do in order to catch the Rebel Executioner.

"This is you?" Zalstra asked, looking up at Longarm with a steady gaze.

"It is. Here is more identification, if you still aren't convinced."

But Zalstra shook his head. "No, I believe you now. And who is this young woman?"

"My name is Miss Lucy Martin," she answered before Longarm could explain.

"What do you both want?"

"I need to speak to Miss Wallace about what happened the day or two prior to the fire that killed her family up in Virginia City."

"That would do no good," the dairyman said, shaking his long, sad face. "Annie is still very upset."

"I'm sure that she is," Longarm replied. "But it's extremely important that we talk to her. Mr. Zalstra, there could be someone that wants to kill her."

The Dutchman sat down on his little milking stool and clenched his big, knotty fists. Longarm sensed that this was a very good, very uncomplicated man who was really struggling to do the right thing given this sudden and great responsibility of caring for another family's orphaned child.

"Mr. Zalstra?" Longarm said. "Did you hear me say that I think someone is trying to kill Annie?"

"Someone already tried," the dairyman answered in a voice that now shook with fear or anger. "They took a shot at her, but missed."

"When!"

"Yesterday. And last night when I was turning the cows out to pasture, I saw a man with a rifle hiding in the trees. I yelled at him and he ran away." Zalstra shook his head. "I am very afraid for our Annie."

"You should be," Longarm said. "But I can give her protection. I can even hide her if necessary until we catch the men or group of men who are trying to kill her."

There was anguish in Zalstra's voice when he cried, "Why would they kill little Annie? Hasn't she suffered enough?"

"Yes, she has," Longarm said in a gentle, patient voice. "But the reason that someone wants to kill her is because she has some very important information about who might have set the fire that took the lives of her entire family."

"You mean it wasn't a cat?"

"I don't think so," Longarm said. "We have good reason to believe that someone *deliberately* set fire to the Wallace mansion out of vengeance . . . or madness."

"Who would do that?"

"That's what we hope Annie can tell us," Longarm said. "Mr. Zalstra, it's real important that we talk to her right now and take her away to be protected until this killer is caught and justice done."

The Dutchman thought about this for several minutes, then slowly nodded his head. "Maybe next time they don't miss with that rifle, huh?"

"That's right," Lucy said. "I think that we have to make sure that there isn't a 'next time.' "

Zalstra led them out of the barn and across his yard. Their house was surrounded by a picket fence and gardens lush with ripening squash, tomatoes, carrots, and peas. There was also a flower bed filled with roses blooming in colorful profusion.

The house itself was made of sawn lumber and had a porch. When they entered the home, Longarm could smell stew cooking, and he only had to glance around to see that this dairy family was prospering. There was a piano, nice rugs on the floors, and china cabinets filled with knickknacks of every description. Family portraits and original but somewhat amateurish oil paintings covered the walls. All in all, the Zalstra home was clean and comfortable.

Mrs. Zalstra came out of the kitchen wearing her apron, but Annie was nowhere to be seen. Longarm suspected that the anxious woman had told her to go to her bedroom and stay there until she was called.

"Mildred, this man is a United States marshal."

"He doesn't *look* like one to me," she said, eyeing Longarm suspiciously. "And who is the woman?"

Once again, Longarm and Lucy were forced to make introductions and produce documents. It took almost fifteen more minutes before Mildred Zalstra was convinced that they had not come with sinister intentions.

"I need to talk to Annie right now," Longarm explained. "We feel that her life is in very serious danger but that she can help us find the man responsible for burning down her house and killing all the rest of her family."

"Annie would have told us if there was such a man," Mildred firmly declared.

"Please," Longarm told her, "let me speak to the

girl. After that, I might have to take her away for a while.''

"No!''

"Yes,'' Longarm said, "but only for a short time and in order to save her life.''

Mildred whirled and rushed back into her kitchen, but she called for Annie to come out. When the girl appeared a few moments later, Longarm saw that Annie was shy and afraid. She was a pretty girl, slender, with dark brown hair and long eyelashes. Longarm was quite sure that Annie would one day be quite a lovely woman, if she lived that long.

He introduced himself, as well as Lucy, to the girl before adding, "Annie, first, we are very sorry about your family. But we are trying to figure out what might have caused that fire.''

"A cat,'' she whispered. "His name was Mouser.''

"I see,'' Longarm said, nodding with understanding and doing his level best not to further upset Annie. "I understand that a friend of your father's named Allen was staying with you. Was Mouser *his* cat?''

Annie shook her head, and Longarm could tell that, despite his best efforts, she was on the verge of tears.

"Annie,'' Lucy said, stepping between them and bending over until she and the girl were on the same eye level, "was this friend of your father named Mr. Allen? Or was Allen his *first* name?''

"I don't know.''

"What did he look like?''

Annie sighed, then looked to Mr. Zalstra, who nodded with encouragement. "Please answer their questions, Annie. They are trying to help.''

"Mr. Allen was nice. He brought me and my brothers presents and he laughed a lot.''

"Do you know if he had been a friend of your father's for a long, long time?"

"I'm not sure," Annie said. "They met during some war. They used to talk about it all the time, but no one else in the family was allowed to listen. Sometimes, I heard them arguing, but they never got too mad."

"I see. Can you describe Mr. Allen?"

"He was big and heavy. He didn't have much hair on his head."

"That's good!" Lucy said. "Was he older or younger than your father?"

"Younger."

"Did he . . . did he have anything else that sort of made him different-looking?"

Annie nodded. "He had a limp, and he used a cane with a silver eagle on the top. And he wore a big diamond and gold ring."

"On which finger?" Longarm asked.

"This one," Annie said, pointing to the ring finger of her right hand. "It had six little red rubies around one big diamond."

"Was he there on the day that you left to go stay overnight with your friends?"

"Yes. He told me that he would be leaving, but not until I came home. He promised me another present."

Lucy and Longarm exchanged penetrating glances, both knowing that this was very likely the Rebel Executioner.

"Annie," Longarm said, "did you see Mr. Allen *after* the bad fire?"

Tears welled up in her eyes and she sniffled. "I think he was burned up too!"

Longarm was finished with asking questions for now. The girl was becoming too upset, and besides, he had heard enough to know that this was likely the man that they were after. Now they not only had a name, but also an excellent physical description.

Furthermore, he was now pretty certain that Mr. Allen, or whatever his real name was, had been present on the night of the fire. It was possible that he had actually decided to leave the Wallace household earlier than planned. Or he might even have panicked and run away during the fire and been too afraid or ashamed to reappear. But in all likelihood, it was Allen who had started the fire and who had also tried to ambush this frightened and upset child.

"Annie," Longarm said, "we think that Mr. Allen and not a cat started the fire. And remember how someone shot at you yesterday?"

"Yes."

"We are afraid that it is this same man and that he wants to kill you so that you can't tell anyone about him. That's why we need to take you away to someplace *safe*. Someplace where no one can find or hurt you until we have found and talked to Mr. Allen."

"No, please! I don't want to leave here!"

Mildred Zalstra wrapped Annie in her comforting arms. "We take care of her, by golly!"

"No," Longarm said. "We believe that Mr. Allen, or whatever his name is, has killed a lot of people. He is a very dangerous man. You wouldn't be able to protect Annie . . . but I can and I will."

Mildred kept shaking her head back and forth.

"Mr. Zalstra," Longarm said, "I'm sorry but we *have* to take Annie for her own good. You saw my badge and my identification. You even saw the letter giving me the full power of the law to do whatever I think is best. Now, I can go back into town and get the marshal, but that would only complicate things and probably upset Annie even more. Help me help save Annie.''

That was just about as long a speech as Longarm had ever made, but it was also just about as important as any he'd ever made. The Dutchman toed the rug with his heavy boots, and finally he dipped his chin in agreement.

''They will protect her, Mildred. We cannot do that so good. Annie has to go with them.''

Gripped by a terrible inner conflict, the woman shuddered, but finally pushed Annie away from her saying, ''Get your things and go with these good people, Annie.''

''But I don't want to go!''

''You have to go. Soon, you will come back here to live with us until you grow up big and strong. I promise this.''

To her credit, the girl obeyed, and after a tearful farewell outside, she climbed into the carriage.

''You protect her with your life,'' the Dutchman warned. ''If she dies, I hold *you* to blame!''

''She won't die, Mr. Zalstra. I swear that she will be all right and that we will bring her back to you as soon as we can.''

''Where are you taking her?''

''I . . . we are taking her to Reno,'' he said. ''I have a friend by the name of Miss Carole Shaw. She is a newspaper reporter there, and that's where Annie will be kept in hiding until this is finished.''

''Carole Shaw?''

''Yes. She works for the *Reno Daily News*. She has a nice house and—''

''Custis!'' Lucy exclaimed. ''Why—''

Longarm ignored Lucy's outburst, and finished what he'd started to tell the big Dutchman. ''A nice house where Annie will be safe and can't be found."

"We could come to visit?"

"Any Sunday. You just come and see Annie any Sunday."

"I find this house and we be there next Sunday," the dairyman vowed. "Next Sunday, Annie!"

After that they drove off, and it wasn't until they turned off on the road north to Reno that Lucy hissed, "Why on earth did you do that?"

"I have my reasons," Longarm said. "But I'm not about to explain them right now."

Lucy flushed with anger, but she was plenty smart enough to know that, whatever reasons Longarm had, they could not be given in the presence of this very frightened fourteen-year-old girl.

Chapter 11

On the road north to Reno, Longarm tried to engage Annie in conversation, but had little success. That did not surprise him, for he had never been any good talking to children because he shared almost nothing in common with them. Lucy, on the other hand, proved to be a wonder with kids. She soon had Annie smiling about pets they'd both had, and then they talked about flowers and birds and all sorts of things that pretty much bored Longarm.

But it was good to hear them laughing, and it was well after dark by the time they arrived in Reno. Longarm still hadn't figured out where they were going to hide Annie, but Lucy had already figured that one out.

"Wait until you see our hotel," she said to Annie. "It's called the Truckee House, and it is the newest and nicest place in the whole town."

"Really?" Annie asked. "I'll be staying there with you?"

"Why, sure!" Lucy exclaimed, catching Longarm by surprise. "Custis will get another room so that you and I can have our privacy."

She looked at Longarm. "That *will* be all right, won't it, darling?"

"Yes, that will be just fine," he heard himself reply. "We'll get adjoining rooms."

"That will be perfect. And every evening we'll dress up and go out to have a nice dinner."

"Him too?" Annie asked, still suspicious of anyone whose face was all banged up and who was sporting puffy lips and a black eye.

"Yes," Lucy said, "whenever he can."

Longarm supposed that the Truckee House was as safe a place as any to keep the girl. Because it was so plush and expensive, it was well protected. And their rooms were on the second floor, so that anyone trying to get to Annie would have a difficult time both reaching her as well as escaping. Longarm decided it was time to send a long-overdue telegram to Billy Vail telling him about Annie and his hunches. He would request a federal officer or two to guard Annie and Lucy while he was trying to ferret out the Rebel Executioner whose name they now believed was Allen.

Longarm didn't know where to take the carriage and horses, so he picked the livery nearest to their hotel, and paid the owner five dollars to remove their harness and board the horses for a couple of nights until he had time to notify Dan De Quille what was happening. He also needed to get ahold of Carole Shaw and fill her in on the events of the past few hectic but productive days on the Comstock Lode.

After leaving their horses and carriage, Longarm and Lucy escorted Annie up Virginia Street, careful to keep the little girl between them. Longarm had taken great care to make sure that they had not been followed from the Zalstras' dairy, but one could never be entirely certain because a really skillful tracker could never be shaken.

"Good evening!" Murphy the porter said as they swept into the lobby of the Truckee House. Then, recognizing Longarm despite his battered appearance, he exclaimed, "My gosh, Mr. Long! What happened to you?"

"Long story. No pun intended."

"Here, let me help you with those bags."

"What I'd rather you do is to see if we can get a pair of adjoining rooms," Longarm informed the man. "But they *must* be on the second floor and facing Virginia Street rather than the back alley."

"I'm sure that can be arranged," the porter said, marching over to the registration desk, where a hurried conversation ensued. It only took a few moments for the arrangements to be made. Then, Longarm, Lucy, and Annie followed the porter up the winding stairway to the second-floor balcony.

"Right down the hall this way," Murphy said, handing Longarm several written messages.

"Gosh," Annie exclaimed, pausing to stare at the immense chandeliers and the beautiful lobby below. "I've never seen *anything* so grand!"

"I told you it was a very special place," Lucy said. "You're going to love staying here with Custis and me."

"Will we be staying here very long?"

"Perhaps a week."

"But how will my aunt and uncle find me if you told them that I'd be staying with Miss Shaw?"

"We'll take care of that," Longarm promised.

Once they were situated in their new and adjoining rooms, they went downstairs and had an excellent dinner before retiring. Longarm inspected the door locks, and warned Lucy to also use the chain for added protection.

"I'm going out for a few minutes," he told her.

For the first time, Lucy showed concern. "Must you?"

"Yes. The messages I received were from Miss Shaw. She's nearly frantic, and I must talk to her at once. Also, I'm going to wire my Denver office and get us some protection."

"Good!" Lucy exclaimed. "That would sure give me some extra peace of mind."

"I should be back within two hours."

"Wake me up when you return."

Longarm kissed her and whispered, "Remember what I showed you about using that derringer?"

"I do," Lucy answered. "And you had better believe that it is loaded and will be resting under my pillow when Annie and I retire."

"Good!" Longarm kissed her again.

Lucy stepped out into the hallway with him. "Do you think that the Zalstras are also now in danger?"

"I am concerned about their safety. That's one of the reasons I've got to telegraph for additional help. My boss can give them federal protection by tomorrow afternoon."

"But what if that's too late!"

"What else can we do?" Longarm asked. "Mr. and Mrs. Zalstra aren't fools. They know that someone has been out to their dairy and has tried to kill Annie. I didn't have to tell them that the very same person could very well try to enter their house and kill everyone.

Mark my word, Lucy, that couple will not be easy victims. We just have to hope that the Rebel Executioner doesn't strike the Zalstras tonight because, by tomorrow night, they'll be under federal protection.''

"What about Carole Shaw? You told the Zalstras that—''

"I know what I said." Longarm expelled a deep breath. "I'll move Carole out tonight. Once she is relocated and safe in hiding, I'll spend a little time waiting at her house just in case our killer comes calling.''

"If he comes to Carole's house, it can only mean that he has already been to the Zalstras and killed them!''

"Lucy, we're doing the very best that we can. We need a little luck and then I'll put an end to this lunatic.''

"You'll capture him?''

"No," Longarm said, deciding that he could no longer skirt the truth. "I've been asked to *kill* him.''

Lucy bit her lower lip, then said, "I have no problem with that. Just make sure that you have the right man.''

"There'll be no mistaking his intentions, and Annie's description was pretty complete." Longarm hugged Lucy and whispered, "After I send the telegram and help arrives tomorrow, the danger will have passed and the rest will be a waiting game.''

"With poor Annie as the bait to our trap?''

"I'm afraid so," Longarm admitted. "But that can't be helped. If the Rebel Executioner isn't stopped, the likelihood is that other women and children will be murdered. It's got to end *here*, Lucy. I told you that this was not going to be easy. I warned you of the dangers.''

"But not that a little girl would become bait for our trap!''

Longarm could only shrug his broad shoulders. "I'll be back as soon as I can. Just lock and chain your door and keep that derringer handy. I'll also slip Murphy some extra money and warn him that there could be an intruder and to be especially vigilant anytime I am gone.''

"All right," Lucy said, taking a deep breath. "I'm sorry that I—"

"Don't be," Longarm interrupted. "You've been very brave and helpful up to this point. I don't know what I would have done out at the Zalstra place if you hadn't been there to smooth things. I'd probably have had to fight Mr. Zalstra and then his wife in order to get Annie out of that danger."

"Hurry back," Lucy pleaded.

"I will."

Longarm went directly to the telegraph office, which was down at the Union Pacific Train depot. After seeing Longarm's badge and identification, the sleepy telegraph operator fired off Longarm's message to Denver. The telegram was marked "urgent," and Longarm paid a hefty price to insure that it was delivered to Billy's house instead of to an empty office.

"Here," he said, giving the telegraph operator an extra five dollars before leaving. "I'm staying at the Truckee House. If there is a return message, I want it delivered immediately to the front desk."

"Yes, sir. What happened to your face, Marshal Long?"

"I stepped into a ring when I shouldn't have."

The telegraph operator's face lit up like a lamp. "Why, I'll bet you're the mystery man that whipped Hammerin' Hank Cutter's butt up in Virginia City a few days ago!"

"Just take care of that telegram," Longarm said before he hurried away.

"I heard that it was the fight of the century!" the man shouted as Longarm dashed off into the night. "And I'd have given *anything* to see it!"

Longarm realized he didn't even know where Miss Shaw lived, so he went to the newspaper office and got lucky. A typesetter was working the late shift, and after Longarm finally managed to convince the man that he was indeed a federal marshal, he was able to obtain Carole Shaw's address. It took only a few minutes to reach her house on Arlington, and the lights were still burning brightly.

"Custis!" she cried when she recognized him standing on her porch. "I could just *kill* you!"

"Wait your turn," he said dryly as he stepped inside her house. "Carole, I haven't much time to talk, so just listen and then do as I say."

"I don't like the sound of that."

"You need to leave this house for a while," he said, "because I'm hoping that the Rebel Executioner is going to come calling at your door in the next day or two."

While Carole was still in shock, Longarm explained everything. After realizing her danger, the woman packed and was gone in an hour.

Longarm turned out the lights and waited in Carole's house until almost two o'clock in the morning. Then he decided that no one was coming and that it was more important that he return to the Truckee House in order to be able to protect Lucy and Annie. He was dead tired and hurting all over a half hour later when he finally mounted the hotel staircase and entered his room.

Lucy was waiting, and she rushed into his arms. "Thank goodness you are back! I've been so worried."

"Any problems?"

"None at all. Annie and I talked for an hour or two

before she fell asleep on my bed. She's a wonderful girl, Custis. Scared, but brave and very smart.''

"Is she having trouble accepting the fact that the loss of her family was due to some crazed killer rather than an accident caused by a cat overturning a lamp?''

"Yes, she is,'' Lucy admitted. "And we talked quite a bit about that. Annie wanted to know about the war because her father forbade anyone to ever mention it in their house. I told her that there were still a lot of men who had never put the war behind them, and that there were a few that had even been driven to madness by the conflict.''

"Good,'' Longarm said. "She needs to understand those sorts of things, and it sounds like you were meant to be the one to explain them to her.''

"Let me help you off with that shirt,'' Lucy said. "I think I'll leave the door open between our rooms and then I'll sleep with you.''

"I'm afraid I'm so sore and tired tonight that sleeping is *all* you'll be able to do with me.''

"That's enough. Just having you here with us gives me a great sense of relief and comfort.''

Longarm let her undress him and help him into bed. He knew that he should have stayed in bed all day, but if he had, he would never have gotten Annie to safety and been able to warn the Zalstras about someone willing to kill them in order to kill the child. And so, yes, it had been a hard, hard day, but one well worth the extreme discomfort and effort.

He awoke late and alone in bed, with the sun streaming through the windows. Grunting with pain from the blows he'd taken from Hank Cutter, Longarm stumbled over to the front window and rubbed his eyes while gazing

154

down on Virginia Street. Suddenly, he saw the glint of sun striking metal on the opposite building's rooftop. Longarm threw himself sideways as a rifle boomed and his window shattered. Keeping to the floor, Longarm scrambled over to his bed and tore his six-gun from its holster. By the time he could return to the blown-out window, the rifleman had disappeared.

A few moments later, Lucy and Annie burst through the adjoining door, and when they saw the shattered glass and Longarm with a gun in his hand, they both knew that the killer had followed them to Reno.

It took a little while for Longarm to calm Lucy and Annie down, and he tried to ease their fears by saying, "This madman must be very desperate or he wouldn't have tried such a bold move right in the middle of town during broad daylight."

"But if he's that desperate, shouldn't we be all the more worried?"

"It will be all right," Longarm said with considerably more assurance than he felt inside. "I'll go see the local marshal, and I'm sure that he can spare a deputy or two until the federal officers arrive to help protect you."

"I wish you wouldn't leave us alone again," Annie said. "I'm getting scared."

"Tell you what," Longarm said, "I'll send for the marshal. In fact, it wouldn't surprise me if he's on his way right now. Someone must have alerted him to this shooting. That being the case, why don't we just sit tight and wait for him."

Longarm's hunch was correct. Marshal Tom Oatman was a hard and grim-faced man of medium height and build with a long, flowing mustache. Probably in his mid-forties, he was missing most of his right ear, and a prominent and puckered knife scar ran from that mutilated ear diagonally across his face to disappear into his scalp, giving him a very distinctive streak of white hair. The man was all business, and he listened with a disapproving frown as Longarm explained all about the Rebel Executioner and the trouble they were now facing in order to protect Annie Wallace.

"You should have come by and told me all this from the start," said Oatman with annoyance.

"I know," Longarm agreed. "But up until yesterday, I hadn't a clue as to who I was trying to catch. I didn't even have any proof that all these killings weren't really just tragic coincidences. And I'm still not sure that there isn't more than one man involved in these executions."

"Well," Oatman growled, "I think the best thing would be to place this girl into protective custody."

"Not in a jail cell!" Lucy protested, drawing Annie up tight against her.

"It'd be for her own good, ma'am."

"Thanks," Longarm said, "but no, thanks."

"Look," Oatman said, his eyes flashing. "I'm the marshal of this town and I've been appointed to keep the peace and to preserve and protect life. Now, if I say that the girl belongs under my protection, that's the way it's damn sure going to be!"

"You're dead wrong about that," Longarm said with an edge creeping into his voice. "I'm the superior authority here, and the girl is staying with me in this hotel room until I decide that there is a better place."

Oatman blanched with anger, and his hand actually moved toward the gun holstered on his hip.

"Don't be stupid," Longarm said, stepping in close and clamping his hand on the lawman's wrist. "We're supposed to be working *together*, not fighting each other."

"You haven't even tried to work with me," Oatman snapped. "If it hadn't been for that rifleman taking a shot at you, I *still* wouldn't know what the hell is going on here!"

"That's true enough," Longarm admitted, realizing he did not like Oatman. "But if you really want to protect someone, I'd suggest you guard Miss Carole Shaw. Hide a man in her house at night and see if you can't earn your pay by capturing her would-be assassin."

Oatman backed away in a fury. "You feds come into a town and think you are God Almighty Hisself! Well, you aren't, gawddamnit! Nobody asked you to come here, and I'm telling you that I won't have you staying in this hotel endangering the other guests."

"What you tell me doesn't mean squat," Longarm snapped. "Now get the hell out of my sight."

Oatman shook with anger, and he jabbed a forefinger at Longarm saying, "You'll be hearing from me, Mr. Long! Gawdamned if you won't!"

"If you push me too far," Longarm warned, "I'll have you arrested and hauled before a federal judge who will throw you in a federal penitentiary for obstruction of justice."

Oatman spun on his heel and shot out the door, slamming it so hard that the pictures jumped on their walls.

"That man is insane!" Lucy cried. "He was ready to go for his gun."

"I know," Longarm replied. "There are a lot of bad local lawman running loose, and Tom Oatman ranks right up there with the worst that I've ever seen. When this business is finished, I think I'll check up on his background and see if he can't be removed from office. It's a risky business because he was appointed by local officials, who usually hate federal officials messing with local issues. But in this case, I think it would be appropriate."

Longarm allowed the hotel staff to clear away the shattered window glass while he took Lucy and Annie back down to the dining room for a late breakfast.

"So what is going to happen next?" Lucy asked, hugging the silent and withdrawn child.

"Well," Longarm said as Dr. Maxwell burst into the hotel dining room, spotted Longarm, and came hurrying over in his direction, "I think it's safe to say that we're just about to find out."

"May I join you?" the doctor asked, slightly out of breath.

"Of course." Longarm introduced Annie, and then he motioned to the waiter to bring the physician coffee and a menu.

"You look upset," Lucy said to the doctor.

"I am."

Maxwell turned to Longarm while reaching into his coat pocket and dragging out a clean handkerchief, which he then unfolded. "Here's the slug that I removed from Lester Gorton yesterday. I've weighed and examined it very precisely. The bullet was .45-caliber, same as the gun I found resting in his hand."

"But Lester owned a .36-caliber Navy Colt. This means that the murderer shot Lester with his own .45-caliber revolver, then took the Navy and planted his own .45 in Lester's lifeless hand."

"How is that going to help you?" the doctor asked.

"It probably won't," Longarm said. "Unless we find Lester's .36-caliber in the killer's possession. What I need to do now is to ask Pete Black if he could identify that—"

"I'm afraid that won't be possible."

"Why?" Longarm asked.

"Because someone murdered Pete Black last night in his bed."

Longarm shook his head as if he could rid himself of a very bad dream. Still, it showed that the Rebel Executioner had known that Longarm was a federal marshal on his trail, which explained why the man had felt it necessary to try and ambush him from a downtown hotel rooftop.

"Sixty dollars," Maxwell said. "That's what you promised me for exhuming Gorton's body, and I earned every last cent of it."

"Yes," Longarm agreed, noting a growing fear in Lucy and Annie's eyes as they digested the news of this latest execution, "you most certainly did."

Chapter 12

Longarm took Annie and Lucy upstairs and told them to lock the door. "Lucy, I won't be gone but a few minutes," he explained.

"Where are you going?"

"I have to go to the telegraph office, and then I want to inspect that rooftop directly across the street and see if the man who tried to ambush me left any evidence."

"That's not very likely, is it?"

"It could be if he was sure that he was going to kill me. If he had, no one would have bothered to inspect his ambush spot."

"I'm worried about you, and about us. Do you *have* to go out again?"

"I'm afraid so. I wouldn't go if I weren't very confident that you and Annie will be safe here in this room. After all, half of Reno knows what happened here this morning. Whoever tried to ambush me will be laying low at least until tonight. Just keep your door bolted and chained on the inside and don't let *anyone* inside. Is that clear?''

"Sure, but . . ."

Longarm kissed her quickly. "I expect that federal lawmen will arrive on tomorrow's train or the next day's at the latest.''

"I hope we're still alive to meet them," Lucy said in a tone too soft to be overheard by Annie.

Longarm nodded grimly and headed for the hallway. He tipped Murphy the porter again, requesting that he be especially vigilant and on the lookout for any strangers.

When Longarm approached the registration desk to ask for the same help and consideration, the man behind the counter wasn't the least bit friendly. "You're not a Wyoming rancher at all, are you?" he snapped.

"No, I'm a federal marshal."

"Why didn't you tell us that in the first place?"

"Because it was none of your business then . . . or now.''

"That shooting this morning was very bad for the reputation of the Truckee House. We can't tolerate that sort of thing. No, sir! And I'm afraid that we'll have to ask you—"

"If you are even thinking about telling me to move out, forget it, before I completely rearrange the shape of your nose," Longarm warned.

The desk clerk shrank back, eyes round with fear. "Well, Marshal," he stammered, "that is certainly no way to treat the public!"

"You're not the public," Longarm said. "You're an employee and you're here to serve the patrons of this hotel, which includes me. So just do as I've asked and let's not have this conversation again, all right?"

"Yes, sir!"

"Good," Longarm said before turning to leave the hotel. "I'm glad that we have come to a clear understanding."

The first place that Longarm went after leaving the hotel was the mercantile building located directly across the street. After showing the owner his badge, Longarm said, "As you probably know, someone attempted to ambush me this morning."

"Sure," the storekeeper said. "Everyone is talking about that shooting and very little else. Pretty bold considering it was full daylight, don't you think, Marshal?"

"I do. Do you realize that the ambusher fired from on top of *your* roof?"

"No!"

"Without a doubt he did," Longarm said. "I need to find out how he managed to get up there."

"Well, he certainly didn't come through my store!"

"Do you have a fire escape?"

"Sure, they're now required by the new building codes."

"Show it to me."

The owner escorted Longarm through his store and into a rear supply room. "As you can see, this back door leads into the alley where our stock is delivered every day," he said, pointing to a heavy sliding bolt. "It is always kept locked when not in use."

"Open it."

The owner opened the door and Longarm stepped outside, then walked over to the fire escape saying, "Just stay where you are for a minute."

"What are you looking for?" the man asked from the doorway.

"Boot or shoe prints."

"How would that help you?"

"I don't know," Longarm said, noting that one set and one set only led away from the fire escape, which was the type that was suspended on springs a good ten feet up in the air. They were common and made sense because they were too high to reach by burglars, yet would lower to the ground under the weight of someone who was escaping a real fire. And it was very clear from the marks that this fire ladder had been lowered recently.

"What do you see?" the store proprietor called.

"Looks to me like the boot prints are pointed *away* from the fire escape, and there is an indentation where the ladder rested for a moment before the springs lifted it back up into the air. That means that whoever tried to kill me came down the fire escape but did not use it to get on the roof."

"They *had* to have climbed it to get up there."

"Why? Isn't there a stairway on the inside?"

"Of course! But the man would have had to be *inside* my store."

"I don't see that that would have been so difficult," Longarm replied, returning to the back door. "Show me the inside stairs."

The man directed Longarm to a far corner of the supply room where the light was so dim that Longarm had to strike a match in order to see the stairway.

"For God's sake, be careful with that match," the store owner warned. "One flick of an ash and everything back here could go up like a torch."

"I'm going on up to the roof to have a look."

"You go right ahead. I got to tend my cash register. I got a business here to run, Marshal."

"Sure," Longarm said. "Go ahead."

With the match still flickering, Longarm climbed the

164

stairs, and then pushed open a heavy ceiling door and emerged on the rooftop. The dust was half an inch thick, and the ambusher's tracks matched those that Longarm had already discovered in the alley. He went over to the Virginia Street side and, sure enough, he found fresh evidence of his ambusher. It seemed obvious that the ambusher must have spent a good many hours waiting for a clear shot through Longarm's window. There were a lot of cigarette butts, most of them behind the back of the storefront sign that advertised the mercantile.

"Someone even had coffee and sandwiches up here last night," he said out loud, toeing the ambusher's refuse and looking for anything that would reveal the man's identity.

There really wasn't anything, but Longarm did collect a couple of the cigarette butts. There were a lot of different kinds of cigarette tobacco on the market for folks who rolled their own, but these were machine-rolled cigarettes, far more expensive and easy enough to identify. Longarm spent a few more minutes studying the rooftop, but found nothing. He did, however, take an exact measurement of the boot marks left by the ambusher.

Most often, things like cigarette butts and boot prints didn't amount to anything. They couldn't, for example, be used in court against someone because they were far too common and therefore inadmissible as evidence. But this case was entirely different. Longarm had been appointed his own judge and jury. He alone would decide what evidence was enough in order to execute an executioner.

"Well," the store owner said when Longarm returned to the front of the building. "Did you find anything important?"

"Could be," Longarm said. "Do you smoke store-bought cigarettes?"

"No."

Longarm produced a cigarette butt. "Do you sell this brand?"

"Let me take a closer look at that," the store owner said.

Longarm gave him the butt.

"Yeah, I sell 'em. They're called Wolfsblends."

"I've heard of them. Not too common, are they?"

"No, but we sell quite a few packs every week."

"Give me the names of whoever buys them."

"I don't remember! And even if I did, I don't have the time."

Longarm glanced down at the storekeeper's feet. "I see that you wear boots."

"So what?"

"Lift one up. I want to measure it."

"Well, dammit, anyway! Do you think *I'm* the fella that took a shot at you this morning?"

"We're about to find out."

"Now wait just a damn minute, Marshal! I've bent over backward to be helpful. And I sure wouldn't be so stupid as to try to ambush someone from my own roof-top!"

"Lift your foot up," Longarm ordered, running out of patience.

"No!"

Longarm kicked the storekeeper's legs out from under the man, causing him to land hard on his plank flooring. While he was still dazed, Longarm studied his boot and measured it.

"You're not my man," he said. "Thanks for your help and I'll be by later for that list of men who regularly buy Wolfsblend cigarettes."

"You go to Hell!" the storekeeper shouted.

Longarm stopped at the door and turned back to the dazed and infuriated man. "Someone came into your store, probably before closing time yesterday. I expect you were busy and he just slipped past without you noticing him. He spent the night on your roof and left by the fire escape. Now, that's my *charitable* theory. Would you like to hear my not-so-charitable one that makes you an accomplice to attempted murder of a federal officer of the law?"

Anger and protest died in the man's eyes and he wagged his chubby double chins back and forth. "No, sir!"

"Then you have that list ready for me. And it had better be complete because, if I see anyone smoking Wolfsblend cigarettes in Reno and they are not on your list, then I'll be coming back with a whole lot of tough questions."

"Well . . . well, I'm not the only gawdamn store owner that sells them in this town!"

Longarm figured that was true, but it didn't hurt to twist the screws a little when a man like that became obstinate and uncooperative.

His next stop was the telegraph office, and Longarm composed his message as he proceeded down the boardwalk, ignoring the stares that his presence generated. When he came to the office, Longarm penciled the message out and said, "Please send this to whoever is the marshal in Carson City."

The message was a warning to the marshal and a request that he go out to the Zalstra dairy and look in on them and provide them with constant protection. Longarm offered little explanation, but did say that it was a matter of high national importance authorized by the

President of the United States. That, Longarm figured, ought to generate some action.

"You want to wait for a reply?" the telegraph operator asked.

Longarm *didn't* want to wait, but he knew that he should. "All right," he said, "I'll be back in about fifteen minutes to make sure that my message was received."

Longarm went to see Carole Shaw at her newspaper office just to make sure that she was all right.

"I've just returned from your hotel," Carole said, glancing up from her office desk. "I'm writing up the story right now."

"Just don't put down the reason behind the ambush," Longarm warned.

"Of course not. You know, Lucy is a lot braver than I first judged her to be. And Annie is also quite brave. They're scared, but holding up remarkably well. I'm impressed."

"So am I," Longarm said. "Are you in a safe hiding place?"

"Yes."

"Don't tell me where it is. Don't tell anyone and make sure, when you leave work, that you are not followed."

"I will, don't worry." Carole stood up in her office and began to pace back and forth, just as Billy Vail always did when he was upset or nervous. Maybe, Longarm thought, there was something hereditary in the habit.

"The Rebel Executioner is so close that I can almost *smell* him," Carole insisted. "He tried to kill you, and now he's after me and anyone else that he thinks is butting into his murderous vendetta. Any idea yet who he might be?"

"No," Longarm said truthfully. "But I expect that he is going to act again soon. I don't have the feeling that the man is long on patience."

"Still think there is only *one* man involved?"

Longarm had considered the question all morning, and still couldn't decide. "It could be one man—the one that Annie knows as Allen. But then, it could be several. I'm just not sure."

"Custis," Carole said, "I sure hope you figure it out soon before anyone else is murdered."

"I'm doing my best. I had a visit from Marshal Tom Oatman this morning up in our hotel room."

"I bet *that* was fun."

"Not exactly," Longarm said. "We had a major difference of opinion. I had to pull a little rank on him and he wasn't a bit happy."

"He's always going off half-cocked, but he has a badge to hide behind."

"What do you mean?"

"I mean that he is mean! He's got a violent nature and quick temper that gets him into trouble. I've covered stories of some of the men he has arrested and beaten."

"Why do the leaders of this town stand for someone like that?"

"Because he keeps the peace," Carole explained. "Nobody wants to get crossways of Marshal Tom Oatman. If you're his friend, things are fine. But if you are his enemy. . . ."

Carole didn't have to finish for Longarm to understand her meaning. "Do you know anything about his background?"

"Like what, for instance?"

"How did he get that terrible scar and missing ear?"

"He got it in a knife fight down in New Orleans many years ago."

"But no one knows that for sure."

"No," Carole admitted. "What are you driving at?"

"Like you, I'm a pretty good judge of human nature, and Oatman is rotten to the core. I'd like to see his background investigated and then have him removed from office before he really hurts or even kills someone."

"Listen," Carole said, "please don't let yourself get sidetracked. Let's get the Rebel Executioner and *then* let's see what can be done with Marshal Oatman. All right?"

"Yeah," Longarm said, "but I sure hate to see such viciousness in a lawman. It taints my entire profession."

They talked for another half hour, and then Longarm headed back to the telegraph office. The operator was standing at his door waving a telegram, and he looked so upset that Longarm actually ran the last twenty yards to meet him.

"What is it?"

"Marshal, I got some real *bad* news."

Longarm felt his heart sink because he knew what the news would be. And sure enough, when he read the telegram, it confirmed his worst fears. Mr. and Mrs. Zalstra had died in a raging fire that had consumed their house early that morning.

"Gawdammit!" Longarm roared in anger and frustration, wadding up the telegram and hurling it into the sky.

The telegraph operator was about to say something when his key started to clacking and he bolted back inside shouting, "Don't run off, Marshal Long. This one is also coming over the line from Carson City!"

Longarm was so upset he wanted to bash his already

bruised fists into the wall. He should *never* have allowed that couple to remain on their farm. On the other hand, he'd known that he'd have had to whip and then tie them both up before they'd have left their lovely home and herd of dairy cows.

"Marshal! This might be real important!"

Longarm took the telegram and scanned it quickly. It was from Marshal Richard Waterford of Carson City, and it said that a boy living on the farm next to that Zalstra dairy had seen and could identify the arsonist who had burned up the Zalstra house. Apparently the boy had been irrigating some pastures, and had seen the man leave the dairy and get onto a large black gelding that had three white stockings and a blaze the full length of its face. The arsonist had not seen the boy but had trotted north, toward Reno, just as the flames were starting to pour out of the house and its windows were exploding from the inferno inside.

"Mister," Longarm said. "Have you seen a horse that fits this description before?"

"Well, I . . . yeah, I have!"

"Who owns him?"

"Clive Allen. He has a little shack just south of town. It's on the way to Carson City, and you probably passed it a bunch of times."

"How far south?"

"Only about a mile. It's off to the west against the Sierra foothills. You'll see a cabin surrounded by huge cottonwood trees. He seems to have spending money, but no one has ever figured where it comes from. Allen has no family and not many friends. He raises pigs and chickens, and just comes into town once a week or two."

"Does he have any hired help?"

171

"I don't know, but I can't imagine he does. I delivered a horse to his place once and didn't see a need for anyone. Everything you see on the Allen place is sort of worn out."

"Did you go into the house?"

"No, he made sure that we did our business in the yard."

"Thanks," Longarm said, cutting off any more questions. "I have one more thing to ask, and that is that I want you to send another telegram to Marshal Billy Vail in Denver."

"Be happy to. You want to write out the message?"

"No," Longarm said, "just say, 'Reno's Clive Allen is the one.' "

"The one what?"

"Never mind. They'll understand." Longarm paid the telegraph operator and hurried away.

He decided not to go up to the hotel room and tell Lucy and Annie of his intentions because it would only worry them sick if they knew he had finally found the Rebel Executioner—provided, of course, that Allen fit Annie's description of the man who had stayed at her house just before it had been burned down.

Longarm ran over to the nearest stable and crammed ten dollars into the fist of the surprised liveryman. "Here! I need to rent your best saddle horse right now!"

"Yes, sir! You want him saddled and bridled too?"

"Hell, yes!"

"It's just that you seem in such an all-fired hurry that I thought. . . ."

"Dammit, I *am* in a hurry!"

"Yes, sir."

Ten minutes later, Longarm was galloping south down Virginia Street. He wished he had a rifle, but hoped that it wouldn't be necessary. Longarm was dead certain that he finally had his man.

All at once Longarm realized that Clive Allen could not have burned down the Zalstras' Carson City home early this morning and also been the Reno ambusher waiting up on the mercantile's roof all night smoking Wolfsblend cigarettes.

Dammit, that means there are at least two of the murdering sonsabitches!

Chapter 13

Longarm had no trouble spotting the Allen shack, but he rode on past its turnoff for about a mile, and when he came to a stand of timber, he reined his horse west into the rugged foothills. He would come around behind the Allen cabin and try to catch the man by surprise. Longarm knew that his orders were to kill the Rebel Executioner, but he doubted he could do that in cold blood. The idea of ambushing Allen or walking up behind the man and blowing out his brains was a hard one to accept, even given the terrible acts that Allen had committed against innocent men, women, and children.

Longarm was still wrestling with this quandary when he dismounted about fifty yards behind the Allen cabin and tied his horse in the pines. Drawing his six-gun, he began to work his way through the heavy undergrowth. Maybe if he hadn't been so troubled about assassinating Clive Allen, he would have noticed the wire and tin cans filled with pebbles that Allen had rigged up around the back side of his place and then camouflaged with dead branches. But Longarm *didn't* see the wire. He caught it with the toe of his boot, and tumbled headlong into a heavy patch of manzanita brush as the cans began to rattle like an infuriated snake.

Before Longarm could untangle himself, he saw a very large, very fat man with almost no hair and a pronounced limp emerge from his cabin levering a Winchester rifle. Allen fired twice, and the first slug tore into Longarm's left shoulder with such force that he almost lost consciousness. Dragging his gun up, Longarm squinted down the sights of his pistol even as another slug punched through the brim of his hat. Longarm fired three times, and each bullet clipped Allen, slowing but not stopping him.

If Allen had been younger, slimmer, and in possession of two good knees, he would have brained Longarm with his rifle because that was his single-minded intention as the crazy bastard raised his Winchester over his head like a club. That was when Longarm emptied his pistol into Allen's corpulent body.

Longarm must have passed out, because he was awakened by shrill shouting.

"Clive! Clive, where the hell are you?"

Longarm fought off waves of pain and dizziness. He figured he was bleeding heavily. He couldn't allow himself to lose consciousness again or he was a dead man. Longarm raised his head just in time to see Marshal Oatman, gun clenched in his fist, coming his way. The marshal was still calling for Allen, so Longarm knew that the lawman hadn't spotted his accomplice's body, but he would in another second or two. It was a struggle

176

to even raise his gun, but Longarm dragged it up, took aim, and then remembered that he was out of bullets.

A chill ran the entire length of Longarm's battered and wounded body. He figured he had no more than five seconds before he was seen and killed by Oatman. However, five seconds wasn't nearly enough time to reload under the best of circumstances, so Longarm slipped his hand inside his coat, fingers tracing a gold chain that connected his Ingersoll pocket watch to a twin-barreled .44-caliber derringer.

Longarm had to hoist his body up a little to extract the derringer, which was pinned under his weight. Then he cocked the powerful hideout gun and pretended he was dead.

"Oh, no!" Oatman exclaimed when he spotted Allen and Longarm's bloodstained bodies.

Longarm struggled to remain conscious as he heard Oatman fighting his way through the brush and fallen timber, then coming to a stop just a few feet away. He could feel Oatman's murderous eyes and knew that, if he looked up, he would be staring into the barrel of Oatman's drawn six-gun.

"Clive!"

Longarm held his breath, fearing that the marshal might actually lose his mind and begin riddling him with bullets. But instead, Oatman grabbed Longarm and rolled him over.

"You!" Oatman hissed.

"Yep," Longarm replied, eyes snapping open and derringer roaring in the very same heartbeat.

Oatman *was* clutching a six-gun. But it was dangling at his side when the first derringer slug ripped upward, entering his groin and tearing his innards apart. The second slug struck the killer just under his chin and blew out the back of his skull.

Longarm dragged himself over to a slender pine, which he used to help him to his feet. Then he began to wobble down toward Allen's cabin. He could barely stay conscious, and knew that he desperately needed a doctor's attention.

Chickens squawked as he staggered toward the cabin's door, and a pen full of pigs, smelling fresh blood, squealed with high anxiety. Longarm barely noticed any of that as he fell through the cabin door, then crawled over to a table and took stock of his surroundings.

First stop the bleeding, he told himself. *Then worry about the rest later.*

He got the bleeding stopped and, because his mind refused to work any longer, he dragged himself over to Allen's bed and felt himself being spiraled downward into a darkness blacker than Hell.

It was almost a month before Longarm was able to board the Union Pacific heading east for Denver, and he was still feeling weak. But the surgeon sent by the President of the United States of America to repair his shattered left shoulder had assured Longarm that he would have a full recovery. Longarm hoped so. He didn't want any big fuss or attention, and he damn sure didn't want to be promoted into a desk and easy chair.

Regarding all the hoopla surrounding the deaths of Clive Allen and Marshal Oatman, Longarm had let the feds take care of that messy business. An exhaustive background investigation of both men had uncovered the fact that they had each been Civil War officers who had suffered severe injuries on the battlefields. Oatman's "knife scar" had actually been inflicted by a Union cavalryman's saber, while Clive Allen's limp had been the result of a minié ball that had shattered his knee and left him to suffer a lifetime of agonizing pain.

As for which of the pair had committed the most atrocities, Longarm guessed that they would never know the answer to that one—and it really didn't matter.

"Custis, we're returning to Carson City next month," Lucy announced. "Annie wants to make sure that Alexander Dunn is taking good care of her dairy herd."

Longarm was taken completely by surprise. "Dunn quit the Miners Union and his job in the Comstock mines?"

"Yes. He's going to run Annie's dairy until we can make other arrangements."

"I thought that the Welshman had hardrock mining in his blood."

"I don't know," Lucy replied, "but when we offered him the responsibility of taking over Annie's dairy at a miner's high wages, Alexander just couldn't say yes fast enough."

"Lucy," Longarm said, feeling a pang of jealousy, "I suspect *you* had something to do with that decision."

"Oh, Custis, you're my hero—you're even a hero to the President of the United States. The pity is that few others outside your agency and the Justice Department will ever know about it."

"That suits me just fine," Longarm said, wondering how he would most enjoy spending the next three months of his promised vacation on full pay.

It struck him that Lucy and Annie made such a perfectly happy and well-matched pair that Lucy would adopt the child and give her the very best of everything. Maybe, Longarm decided, it would be fun to accompany them back to Carson City, where he would get fat on fresh cream and rebuild his strength feeding and milking dairy cows.

But then, the image of himself perched on a milking stool dodging flying piss and cow shit caused him to laugh right out loud.

A special offer for people who enjoy reading the best Westerns published today.

If you enjoyed this book, subscribe now and get...

TWO FREE
WESTERNS

A $7.00 VALUE—NO OBLIGATION

If you would like to read more of the very best, most exciting, adventurous, action-packed Westerns being published today, you'll want to subscribe to True Value's Western Home Subscription Service.

TWO FREE BOOKS

When you subscribe, we'll send you your first month's shipment of the newest and best 6 Westerns for you to preview. With your first shipment, two of these books will be yours as our introductory gift to you absolutely *FREE* (a $7.00 value), regardless of what you decide to do.

Special Subscriber Savings

When you become a True Value subscriber you'll save money several ways. First, all regular monthly selections will be billed at the low subscriber price of just $2.75 each. That's at least a savings of $4.50 each month below the publishers price. Second, there is never any shipping, handling or other hidden charges— *Free home delivery*. What's more there is no minimum number of books you must buy, you may return any selection for full credit and you can cancel your subscription at any time. A TRUE VALUE!

Mail the coupon below

To start your subscription and receive 2 FREE WESTERNS, fill out the coupon below and mail it today. We'll send your first shipment which includes 2 FREE BOOKS as soon as we receive it.

Mail To: **True Value Home Subscription Services, Inc.** P.O. Box 5235
120 Brighton Road, Clifton, New Jersey 07015-5235

YES! I want to start reviewing the very best Westerns being published today. Send me my first shipment of 6 Westerns for me to preview FREE for 10 days. If I decide to keep them, I'll pay for just 4 of the books at the low subscriber price of $2.75 each; a total $11.00 (a $21.00 value). Then each month I'll receive the 6 newest and best Westerns to preview Free for 10 days. If I'm not satisfied I may return them within 10 days and owe nothing. Otherwise I'll be billed at the special low subscriber rate of $2.75 each; a total of $16.50 (at least a $21.00 value) and save $4.50 off the publishers price. There are never any shipping, handling or other hidden charges. I understand I am under no obligation to purchase any number of books and I can cancel my subscription at any time, no questions asked. In any case the 2 FREE books are mine to keep.

Name _____

Street Address _____ Apt. No. _____

City _____ State _____ Zip Code _____

Telephone _____

Terms and prices subject to change. Orders subject to acceptance by True Value Home Subscription Services, Inc.

Signature _____
(if under 18 parent or guardian must sign)

12178-9